Antonija Mežnarić

MISTRESS OF GEESE

Mistress of Geese

Publisher: Shtriga

ISBN
ebook: 978-953-8360-09-1
paperback: 978-953-8360-10-7

Author: Antonija Mežnarić
Edited by: Vesna Kurilić
Cover photo: Mojca Brenko-Puzak

Ebook published in Rijeka, 2020
Paperback published in Rijeka, 2021

The Lottery was first published as *Lutrija* in *Ubiq*, issue 25, 2019
Mistress of Geese was first published as *Gospodarica gusaka* in the anthology
Decameron 2020: Priče iz karantene, 2020

First edition

shtriga.com
shtrigabooks@gmail.com
@shtrigabooks

Antonija Mežnarić

MISTRESS OF GEESE

SHTRIGA

TABLE OF CONTENTS

Make a Toast to Spring

THE ELEVATED, ELEGANT HORNS made a crescent impression above the wearer's head, smooth and glistening in the golden hour. They were the most impressive part of the already quite amazing, albeit morbid mask. Jelena wanted to stop staring, but couldn't really help herself. Nor could her friends.

"Do you think it's real? I mean, made from a real animal's head," Borna asked, unabashedly checking out the horns, his curly black hair falling over his face. They were not the only ones at the convention gaping at this peculiar cosplayer. Jelena vaguely remembered when, a few years back, a girl wore impossibly high, hoof-shaped platform heels, as a part of her satyr costume. Have people recognized something inherently animalistic in Istrakon, and were now dressing accordingly, or was she just reading too much into it? Probably the latter.

Tina rolled her eyes. "It's as real as a bellman's mask." She was the only one not really impressed or acting like it. Jelena supposed it was probably because, as a who-knows-which-generation of Kastavians, all of the men in Tina's family, from the old ones to the toddlers, were a part of the time-honored pagan bellmen tradition. In their masks and sheep hides, with a great cattle bell on their butts, they would dance the winter evils away and bring out spring. The subject usually brought out a lot of pettiness in Tina, since she was excluded from that same tradition because of her genitals. Jelena wasn't sure why anyone would want to be a part of the drunken winter procession, beating her own butt with a bell until it turned purple, but it was what Tina wanted and what she couldn't have. Now, though, she was acting like everyone committed some great offense against her family just for admiring the cosplayer.

Jelena knew all the bellmen's masks because one couldn't live in Rijeka without knowing them. But this one was still hard to put into perspective, for multiple reasons. It wasn't like Grobnik's bull skulls, nor Kastav's grotesque animal masks made of wool, with big grins, open jaws or lolling tongues. Even when you could recognize the animal—like bears, lions, wolves—it was stylized, not realistic. This one, though—it looked like someone had cut off the bull's head, scooped out the gooey insides, brain and skull, and then stuck their own head into it. It made for a pretty terrifying sight. Especially since the rest of the costume were some really mundane clothes. A band t-shirt—not Dimmu Borgir, like Jelena would choose with that mask, but Koktelsi, a small local band known for their carnival and village feast music—jeans and Chucks. There was, however, the added accessory in the form of a long bullwhip, wrapped through the jeans' loops in place of a belt.

"Just sayin', you know. There's a reason the bellmen are protected by UNESCO," Tina still droned in the background.

Jelena didn't really listen to half of what Tina was saying, sipping her watered-down beer, bought at the 'Bree Inn'—a makeshift bar built only for this purpose inside the convention hall. "What are they even cosplaying?" She asked what she was curious about the most. Everyone appeared to be in agreement that the cosplayer was male, because of the build—tall, muscular, broad shoulders—but she didn't want to jump to any conclusions.

"I think it's some game," Borna answered, deep in thought. "League of Legends, I think?"

"That's a minotaur," Elrond—also known as Jakov by only the closest of friends—said, already scrolling on his phone. "And, besides, it looks completely different, see."

"Okay, so it's some *other* minotaur character," Borna answered.

"It must be something more local. Some fantasy book or story by one of our authors," someone they didn't actually meet, but who was standing close by and obviously listening to their conversation, jumped in.

"Why do you think that?" Tina asked their eavesdropper, a guy in an Alien facehugger t-shirt with long hair like the majority of con-goers. His friends were standing by, but weren't overly interested in joining in the talk.

"That's not any bull's head. It's the Istrian bull—boshkarin. Plus, the whole getup with a Koktelsi shirt? It has to be something local."

That line of thought definitely made sense. They were, after all, in the central town of Istria, Pazin, where its annual sci-fi convention was held. Istrakon even published their own anthology of Croatian scifi and fantasy stories, not that Jelena or her friends cared. So a lot of Croatian genre authors used the opportunity to promote their work. It could very well be some smart marketing ploy. Find someone to wear a pretty damn cool cosplay from your obscure novel, which nobody has read because you're not an international writer, and have people scratch their heads trying to guess who that could be, until someone gathers enough courage to ask.

"Hm, mad respect in any case," Borna said, shrugging.

Tina frowned. "This is ridiculous. I'm gonna go ask."

For a moment, Jelena thought to join her, but she wasn't really keen on getting up from her place at the short retaining wall, opposite of the convention center. The sun was getting down, which meant that, very soon, it would become too cold to simply sit outside. And inside... well, they'd already seen everything that they could at the booths—books, merchandise and accessories—and she didn't really have a lot of money to spend this year (even though she did, in fact, buy herself a Super Mario coaster and, of course, an overpriced Stranger Things t-shirt). She didn't like to stay at the bar for too long simply because drunk people always reserved those spots. So that left the convention programming, which was... well. It didn't matter, though; Jelena loved Istrakon to bits and pieces, regardless of what they did or didn't have to offer.

Tina disappeared inside the stocky building, following the cosplayer.

"Do you think one of us should've followed her?" Elrond asked, fixing his horn-rimmed hipster eyeglasses, the only thing marring his otherwise uncanny similarity to a long-haired Hugo Weaving.

"Why? She'll be fine," Jelena answered. "Or you think the cosplayer won't be okay?"

"Yes, but, will *we* be fine?" Elrond continued. "She's our group's dedicated extrovert."

The three of them looked at each other, then at the courtyard where other groups of people had already formed, drinking, smoking and laughing out loud. Both Elrond and Borna came closer to Jelena, Borna with an exaggerated frightened face. She chuckled, but couldn't really appreciate the joke in full. Not since she saw a group of men eyeing them from their spot on the terrace of the convention center's café, Epolon. The looks weren't exactly hostile, but the group were very obviously locals and you could never be sure with people like that. What they thought of geeks. What they thought of *her*.

She made herself look away, feeling queasy, and it turned out to be right on time to catch Tina's march back.

"Oh, oh," Jelena said, pointing behind Borna and Elrond, "she's back and looks pissed."

Tina joined them with a flushed face, crossing her arms at her chest. "The bastard didn't want to answer me. And not just that. Do you know what he said when I *politely* asked what he was cosplaying? After complimenting his mask?"

Her voice was biting, eyes set in a frown only a teacher could cultivate in a classroom full of rowdy children. It was the face that could make grownups hunch in shame.

"*MOO!*" Tina yelled and Jelena flinched, brushing a bush behind her back.

"No way," Elrond said, trying to hide his snickering. Borna, on the other hand, didn't; he flat out started guffawing.

"That's not funny." Tina, of course, wasn't amused, looking like an angry porcupine with her short-trimmed hair. "I was nothing but polite!"

"It's probably just part of the roleplay," Jelena tried to placate her, "remember all those Cersei cosplayers? We couldn't get near them and their resting bitch faces."

Tina still didn't look overly happy, probably thinking this as a sort of personal insult.

Borna enveloped her in a half hug. Which was always a humorous sight—he was the shorter one, by a whole head. "Sorry, but, I mean, you need to admit this is a tiny bit funny."

For a moment, it looked like Tina would remove him from her vicinity by force, like some unwanted limpet. However, her frown changed into a half smile. "Okay, yeah, a bit."

Crisis averted, Borna stepped away from Tina, all four of them now laughing.

"I still want to punch him in his dick for humiliating me like that," Tina said.

They did actually plan to go to a few lectures in the program. There weren't a lot of interesting topics they could listen to; for Jelena, this wasn't the sort of convention where she wanted some deep or intellectual discussion on movies or literature, it was more of a 'get together in the beautiful countryside and drink a lot' type of con. Once she passed Uchka mountain, the natural border between Istria and the rest of Croatia, and came to this forest-riddled hill region, she could easily slip into a more 'village festivities' kind of mood. Why would she want to spend hours listening to capitalist criticism in the Alien franchise, no matter how amazing it was, when there was an idyllic landscape in the background and cheap drinks to help her get lost in oblivion?

However, there was one guy whose lectures they always attended at Istrakon. Not because he was great, or because his topics were something that interested them specifically, but because his lectures were always a hilariously absurd trainwreck of conspiracy theories, which meant a good hour of stand up comedy gold. This year, the topic was the apparent tradition of human sacrifices in Istria, starting from the Bronze Age town Monkodonja where, truth be told, there was a gigantic pit which, historians hypothesized, was used for ritualistic sacrifices. However, the lecture's abstract in the program flyer promised to uncover the hidden truths of rural Istria, hinting that these rituals were still in play. So, of course, when they saw this topic and that lecturer's name on the programming, it wasn't a question what they would be doing in that time slot.

They didn't expect the convention to cancel his lecture at the last moment. Food poisoning, the staff said on Facebook, apologizing profoundly.

"Oh, shit, what now?" Tina proclaimed with a sigh.

There was a quiz they were planning to go to, one of the big, nerdy pop culture games, famous for being extra hard. Which meant it was always packed with competitive geeks. But it wasn't until later in the night, and they'd just lost one hour of something to kill their time with in between. Oh well, an hour of Dixit wasn't that bad, in Jelena's book, and maybe they'll see some of their congoer friends in the game room and get to hang with them.

"What about this lecture?" Borna asked, pointing at the name on the cheaply printed flyer with the programming which Tina held in her hands.

"Aaand, that's also canceled," Elrond said, waving with his phone in the air. Borna looked at the booklet the convention staff had given him with his lanyard, with a face that clearly said, *Why am I even bothering?*

Jelena noticed that the same group of locals was stealing glances towards them, still. What was it that was so interesting in the four of them? They weren't any different than the other little groups littered around the courtyard. That guy with the Alien t-shirt and his friends were basically identical to her group! *You know why they're looking at you,* an annoying voice whispered in her head. It was wrong, it couldn't have anything to do with her. Yet, her skin prickled with a slight discomfort.

"Well, you know what this means," Borna said, wiggling his bushy eyebrows. He took out the small glass bottle with midnight blue liquid in it, shaking it.

"You really think it's time for the big stuff? I'm still on beer," Tina said, watching the bottle doubtfully.

"We need to be cool-headed for the Ultimate Nerd Quiz. You know how insane the questions can get. I can't be drunk for that," Elrond fussed about, the only one of the four who felt like he constantly needed to prove his geek cred.

"Yeah, like we've never done that before," Borna said, with a snicker. "Besides, I'm not saying we need to get shit-faced. Just, you know, a shot to toast our fallen comrades, the lectures about cryptids and the human sacrifices in Istria."

"We could go and listen to the book promotion," Jelena piped in, scrolling. "The author promises to play the ukulele."

"God no, I would rather eat that ukulele than spend my time listening about Croatians in space or whatever the novel is about," Tina said. "Probably vampires. It's vampires, isn't it? Or, even worse, something about local krsniks fighting against ancient evil, because we don't have enough stories about that." She took the bottle from Borna to her hands. "What do you think this is, anyway?"

"Didn't the kind lady say rakija?" Elrond asked instead of answering.

"Actually," Jelena jumped in, racking her brain, "she only said it was a little something homemade, to make us feel like at home."

On Istrakon weekend, the town of Pazin could get fully booked at something like two months in advance. A lot if it was because the town was small, with limited options for renting. A few houses on Airbnb and a too expensive hotel.

So the four of them had to search for nearby accommodation, which meant looking for houses in villages in the greater Pazin area. They ended up finding a quaint, one storey house in the middle of nowhere—the village was in the woods, with, like, four to five other houses, but it was also fifteen minutes by car from Pazin. One of those places where everyone looked at your car as if you'd gotten there by chance, where the cell phone coverage and the internet connection were of a horror movie quality. When they'd passed the first house in the row, a child in the yard had watched them suspiciously, before getting inside his house. That sort of a village.

But the owner of their Airbnb house was a kind and welcoming old woman, although awkward. And not in a 'doesn't know where to fit Jelena in her mental gender brackets', or 'doesn't know how to act around the butchiest of butches Tina, who looked like an American redneck' awkward. Just, talking too fast while trying very hard to make them feel at home, like some of the renters sometimes did.

She'd also gifted them with store bought cookies and homemade alcohol. So, one of the good ones, really.

"Have you ever seen rakija in that color?" Tina asked, putting the bottle in front of her eyes, like it will give up its secrets.

"Who cares? It's homemade, meaning it has to be made from some fruit, probably." Borna didn't sound like he believed that himself. "If not rakija, then some fancy liqueur. Maybe they added some food coloring to make it more interesting." Did people even put food colors in booze? Jelena didn't have the faintest idea. She hoped it wouldn't be one of the questions in the quiz later.

Borna took out the white plastic cups from his backpack and gave one to each of them. They were still drinking like college brats. Well, Borna was, technically, still in college. The others didn't have that sort of excuse. Although, Jelena, who didn't have a lot of money since freelance graphic design wasn't that lucrative, didn't have anything against drinking free stuff from cheap plastic cups.

"I'm drinking only one, for a toast," Elrond warned, like some sort of solemn vow.

"If you get drunk, we can always walk back. And pick up the car in the morning," Jelena proposed. All three of them turned towards her with equal horrified looks on their faces.

"In the middle of the night in the cold?"

"Up the hill?"

"Through the woods?"

They spoke almost simultaneously.

Jelena shrugged. It was a possibility. Not a great one, sure. But still something they could do.

Tina poured two fingers of the mysterious alcohol to each of them. Jelena sloshed hers around. The liquid was oily, thick, with a smell that hit her nose so hard that it dragged out a childhood memory of getting lost in a heavy fog, when collecting chestnuts from the ground in the early autumn mornings.

"To Istrakon!" Borna said, his cup in the air. They all toasted back.

Jelena swallowed her shot and almost spat it out. It was strong, bitter, throat-burning, so much so that she could feel all of her esophagus on fire. She had nothing to compare the taste with, feeling like she'd drunk a shooting star that didn't get the time to cool out.

"Well, that's nasty," Tina was the first one to comment, her face scrunched.

Borna didn't look any better. But he poured himself another one. "What? Do we have anything better to do? Besides, you don't look a gift alcohol in the mouth."

The quiz presenter's head was so swollen it looked like a melon ready to burst out with a chestburster. Or, maybe, with a thousand slimy squirmy maggots, fat on brain juices. She could see it so vividly—there, below his scalp, tiny white bodies were feasting on the organ. She could hear them wriggling: the wet, squishy sound of their mucus-filled forms crawling over each other.

"Hey do you see them eating his brain know this answer?" Voices overlapped, coming out of Tina's mouth. She was sitting so far away, almost on the opposite part of the room and, at the same time, in a chair beside Jelena. These two Tinas overlapped, a blurry image on the camera. "Can you even see the decay the screenshot? Do you recognize the malicious souls movie?"

Jelena blinked, then blinked again, her head full of air. Her vision swam with the motions of a boat rocking on a stormy sea. Her stomach reacted with the same amount of nausea.

"Hey, corruption eats us away, hey," Tina whispered through the herringbone seam on her lips, "I think they are still here, even though they should've left with the bellmen's dance you're way more drunk than I thought."

Jelena leaned towards Tina, wanting so hard to ask her to clarify, to get her fixed in one spot in space, but the other woman just blinked away again. *We didn't drink that much, did we? Wasn't it just two shots of that...*

The room tilted nastily, the abrupt change of perspective bringing up the goo of half-digested food to her throat. Jelena swallowed it down, a part of her aware that she was not in a place where it would be appropriate to puke. She closed her eyes, hoping it would help. She could hear faint sounds of other people talking, laughing, all merging into a white noise of a tuned-down television. She was faintly aware of her body shaking, but also not. It wasn't her body, not really. It was just a bucket in which her mind was hanging on by a loose thread, and she was sure that, when she opened her eyes, she would see that she was in the bed back in the Airbnb, sleeping, and that she'd probably pissed herself while dreaming.

That wasn't fair—a brief flash of thought passed—she fought so hard to make her body her own and not any stranger's. And now it was slipping away from her, again.

"Jelena, Jelena, Jelena..." sudden, recognizable words slashed through, breaking her out of darkness, into the light. People were sitting around her in the hall, turned towards the projection on the screen, their faces completely blank. Not entirely there. Lines whipped off with an eraser. She put her palms against her own face, tracing the edges of the mouth, the bridge of the nose and the arches of the eyebrows with her fingers, just to be sure they were still there.

All she could feel was the plastic sensation of a mask instead of her face. Where was her body? Where did she leave it? A tiny sludge of panic tried to alarm her, but couldn't pass. It was an emotion for the living, not for mannequins. Nothing could happen to her, to this dream shell conjured by nightmares. There was no room for fear, because she couldn't feel.

There were three bodies close at hand, unrecognizable after falling under the eraser. Behind one, a massive shadow made of red pulsing veins stood, one hand on the shoulder of Jelena's faceless friend. She wanted to open her mouth and ask who it was, but forgot that she didn't have movable lips. She should know who that was, shouldn't she? She was somewhere, with someone, doing something. There was a purpose to her. Something she was supposed to do. Or say. Most importantly, she wasn't alone. Where were her friends?

You have none, a shadow said in her ear. She didn't even notice it come closer to her, just a breath caressing her neck. A wet touch of a coarse tongue lapped under her earlobe, teeth nibbling at her throat. She flinched, moving away, or at least that's what her brain planned to do, but her limbs didn't acknowledge it. The white noise hum electrified. Somewhere under it, a vibration snuck, forming words she could understand. "Jelena." It was her name. "Jelena, are you alright?" someone asked.

"She needs to throw up."

"Why are you looking at me...?"

"I feel too drunk to drive, and I know I only had..."

"Did you see that? Did you see how the sky ate the stars? It just, it just... opened up a hole and swallowed it all up, like soup. Lap, lap."

"Jelena, you need to puke! Come on!"

The command was achingly familiar, and it broke through the confusion, making her retch. Her mind suddenly dropped down into her body, hard, after floating outside of it like a tethered soul, almost blown away by the invisible wind. Now, she was all there, on all fours, her eyes so close to the shrubbery she could feel it tickling her face. Her stomach heaved, her neck in a tight hold of someone's cold, wet palm.

"Come on!" She finally placed the voice. Tina, it was Tina holding her there on the grass covered ground with a tiny shrub growing out.

She wanted to say, *I'm trying*, but it came out in the form of retching, followed by slime. A greasy, thick line of blue slime; it almost wasn't a liquid but solid matter. It mapped out her interiors, making her gag even more when she realized she could feel every inch of it passing through her esophagus.

"There's nothing wrong with the sky."

"Why won't you drive then?" Tina's voice was so close it was a shout resounding in Jelena's brain.

"Because... because I don't feel well. I don't... don't see. It's just blurry. All blurry."

"We need to run."

"What?"

"Run, they're coming."

"Who?"

"Jakov, please, do something, he's panicking."

Who's Jakov?, Jelena almost asked, before remembering that Elrond wasn't an actual human name. Her senses were slowly getting into focus—sharpening out her shaking hands, the rancid smell of her bile, her long, honey-colored hair almost getting in the way of the projectile; Tina's polished black boots in the corner of her eye. She still didn't feel like having enough strength to stand up, so she strenuously put everything she had into not falling face-first in her puke instead.

"What are you doing?" Tina again. "Why are you taking off your shirt?"

"Don't you see? This is not my skin! This is not my skin!"

"What? That's your shirt! Borna, you... where are you going?! Wait! Come back!" Pause. "Shit. Do something! Go after him!"

Jelena took a deep breath, full of cold night air, her head clearing up. Finding a new molecule of will, she turned towards Tina, her eyes catching the dark jeans and red flannel first, before rising towards Tina's face. Jelena almost burst out screaming, stopping at the last moment. Tina's eyes—all five of them—blinked in confusion. "Jelena, what's wrong? Don't you freak out, not you too."

Instead of Tina's warm brown ones, the eyes watching Jelena now were two cat's eyes instead, with vertically slit pupils in bright green irises Tina didn't have. Above them, on her forehead, two round, netlike bulbs—eyes of a fly—grew out of the skin of her head, not particularly looking at Jelena or, really, anywhere.

One lonely brown eye was left, but it was in her mouth's usual place, without eyelashes, only eyelids, closing and opening, completely bare. When she talked, the iris would split in half like an egg, showing the dark hole of her mouth, light yellow fluid leaking out. A hint of a tongue moved the white of the eyeball.

"Why are you looking at me like that?" Tina's eye mouthed, her eyeball constricting in a way it shouldn't be able to. Jelena was never as desperate to throw up, riding nausea like a train. But she couldn't, her stomach gaping wide with emptiness. Instead, she just lowered her gaze, avoiding Tina's face.

"Come on, we should try to find a lift to the house. Someone here will help us," Tina said, helping Jelena up. She was so calm, collected. How was she not drunk?

A light from the lamp in the yard hit their backs, Jelena's shadow falling over shrubs, distorting on the branches like it had been impaled. Her eyes firmly fixed to the ground as she limped on, she noticed something else. She jerkingly checked it, just to be sure, since her mind wasn't working well enough to comprehend physics. No matter how hard she looked, though, there was bareness where there should be none.

There was only one shadow showing on the ground.

"Jelena?" Tina's voice was so close that her talking, leaking eye must've been somewhere above Jelena's shoulder, dropping fluid over her. Tina was always so tall, Amazonian, towering over most people. Her strong grip was the only thing now keeping Jelena upright, muscles built with shooting from the compound bow. Perfect for splitting open skulls with bare hands, so that her lost shadow could take a bite out of Jelena's brain with its vaporous canines.

She didn't know where that image came from, but it made her shudder with the need to break out of Tina's grip. It was ridiculous; Tina had been there for her for ages, ever since they were little kids. She was the truck that mauled over every bully that ever tried to get under Jelena's skin, every jerk that tried to misgender or deadname her. Tina was her oldest friend, in fact, even taking care of her in a moment like this one, but it was as if she weren't there at all. As if their whole history, whole friendship, was an evanescent cloud, steadily vanishing into the night air. As if Tina weren't really there; instead, it was someone else wearing her skin, but not completely fitting in it.

"I need... a moment," Jelena managed to tell this stranger holding her, completely alone in the yard filled with curious onlookers, "just, I need to sit."

Tina helped her over to the short wall framing the courtyard of the convention center, very close to where they'd sat and drunk hours earlier. Only hours? Maybe minutes, or maybe days. She couldn't be sure.

She sat down on the wall, the cold seeping under her clothes, freezing her butt. Tina told her not to move, and went towards a group of chattering people who were standing near the door. With her back turned, Jelena finally felt like she could look up without fear of glimpsing at Tina's face. The people she was barely aware of in the background became solid frames, normal-looking, cigarette-smoking, beer-drinking congoers. They were standing above a huge smoking cauldron—warming themselves up—at the same spot where the conrunners had, earlier in the day, shared cooked beans for free to the visitors. The fire under the cauldron was illuminating the scene and grinning faces of gathered people, over dogs that were slowly being cooked inside. A white head of some kind of setter was hanging over the metal rim, eyes completely melted from the skull, dripping on the ground. Someone stirred the boiling water with a huge wooden spoon, before sticking the head back inside.

Jelena wanted to weep, she wanted to rage. Mostly, she wanted to get the hell away from the sight of the dogs getting cooked. This couldn't be happening, but no matter what was real and what not, her brain screamed in a prehistoric dread, shooting her up with adrenaline. It was enough to get up on her legs and let them take her as far away as possible from this place.

From these people with orange faces and hungry mouths.

From Tina, who she couldn't really recognize anymore.

The world spun on its axis, just a flat disk balancing on a cane. The top of the town's belltower came into view and disappeared again, a fixture in the land. At some point she was aware of walking by the stocky medieval castle of Pazin, the darkness obfuscating the zip line over the canyon at its side, but a moment later, houses and old fortification turned into trees and muddy ground. A loud susurration of running water meant that a river was nearby. That wasn't good. It meant she was headed in the opposite direction from where she should be going, if she wanted to go to the rented house. Down instead of up.

Turn around. Which way? She turned and walked uphill, faintly aware of a slippery flight of stairs, which would bring her towards the castle and the town. But now she saw that she had been descending all of that time.

Jelena stopped, turned, fear gripping her in a tight embrace, her eyes screaming for any kind of light to illuminate her path. She continued uphill, only for the world to rotate under her feet, making her descend, again.

A scream tore from her throat, rustling the leaves above her head. She blinked away the tears from her eyes, her sight already limited, even without her crying. Dimly remembering the existence of phones, she dug hers out of her pocket—where was her bag?—and opened the torch app. The light bloomed at one spot, suffocating darkness closing in over the circle of her lamp. Shakingly, she tried to find the path up to the town, the steps she was on just now. But there were none. Just mud, stocky wooden limbs, a murmur of water clicking nearby.

The hint of a bright color on a branch on the left from her called for attention. It was a piece of clothing, hanging loosely, abandoned. Taking it in her hands, she could see the item for what it was—a discarded pair of pants. Her mind drew a blank at that, as if it couldn't really fit what she'd found into the scenery around her. Then a recollection managed to get through the fog in her head. Borna wore this ridiculous cherry color.

The pieces started falling into place. He'd run away somewhere, while she'd been puking, and then Tina had yelled something about him taking off his shirt. Was he running naked around Pazin, in the middle of March? Jelena involuntarily shuddered at the thought, aware of the cold that was embracing her. Getting through her sneakers and socks, under the soles of her feet, climbing up her legs, over her arms, regardless of the leather jacket she wore.

Borna was drunk out of his mind, like her, possibly lost somewhere in the dark, forest-covered canyon, stark naked in the freezing air of early spring. He could slip and fall, break his neck, or he could catch hypothermia and slowly die before someone finds him. She needed to help him, but couldn't even help herself.

What was she even doing here in the first place?

The world spun and spun, just a merry-go-round, a wheel of flame, of burning eyes. There was something in the woods, in the canyon, in the air she breathed in. The piercing melody started following her futile search; a search for what, her mind couldn't really decide. In a moment she would remember Borna, and it would be his name she called in the night, such a small, two syllable word consumed by the shrieking, vibrating music, echoing loudly all around her. A moment later, her ears would finally connect with her brain, and she would understand that the music meant someone else was there, so she should call for help. A shrill vibrato of a wind instrument only mocked her, its player out of her reach, somewhere beyond where the small circle of her artificial light fell.

"Jelena!" she heard somewhere behind her, the familiarity of the voice so disturbingly strange, as if she'd heard it over the phone and couldn't recognize the speaker. But she knew who it was, and it made her only run in the opposite direction, her fear kicking in.

Her heart knew something her brain still didn't comprehend—someone was driving her oldest friend. She couldn't bear to see that walking puppet body, couldn't risk being caught by that thing parading as Tina. So she ran and ran, while the music was crescendoing into a pitch so loud her eardrums were on the verge of shuttering.

Slipping on something wet, her arms met the muddy ground in a painful *thud*, catching her falling body in the last moment before her head could crack open on some rock. Her phone fell out of her hand, rolling out, the light flashing like a disco ball, showing glimpses of something, a kaleidoscope of things—something pinkish, crumpled, left there on the ground, changing with the wood, the roots, the trunks. The light finally settled on a lichen-covered hackberry tree.

Not seeing it didn't mean it wasn't there. Completely aware where she'd seen something discarded on the ground—another piece of clothing, probably—Jelena stood up, her palms stinging, and took the phone back in her hand. She just hoped it wasn't Borna's briefs.

It wasn't. She stood there, light on the ground, and her mind still couldn't comprehend what her eyes were seeing. The background soundtrack continued, her unknown player not getting tired in the slightest, the music nudging her to either move away quickly or take a better look at what she'd found. Crouching, she picked it up—the leathery material stoking her dread. As soon as she touched it, it unfurled—raised in the air, it showed the whole length hidden in the crumpled bundle. A long tuft of curly hair fell from one leathery part and that simple, recognizable piece made her jerk so hard she dropped the thing. Her heart beat louder than the eerie music as light fell on the shedded skin on the ground. She'd had it in her *hands*. She couldn't bear it, didn't want to see the empty space where meat, bones, muscle and organs should be, so she ran away.

Her eyes burned with tears, images flowing wild inside her mind. Borna running alone, shedding his clothes, everything he'd had on, not stopping even when he was naked and when there was only his skin to pull off. The light of Jelena's phone shone on the lonely patches on the ground, showing more she didn't want to see—crimson chunks, dark wet lumps she didn't want to identify. She didn't want to see, and yet, even through blurry tears and patchy light, it appeared her brain could only focus on Borna's discarded body parts.

It wasn't possible, she was hallucinating, this was just her mind playing tricks; how could someone scoop up his liver in his arm to throw it away and then walk further to discard his beating heart? How could someone walk with their guts unfurling on the ground? Leaving their body like bread crumbs for friends to find. It wasn't possible.

Her lungs burned in exhaustion, her body in a complete state of panic, repeating *it wasn't possible* as a mantra, when she finally found the biggest piece of what was left of Borna.

She stopped dead in her tracks. The weeping music wailed, her bones hurt from the sound, or maybe the sight in front of her. Of course, there was no way for her to know that it had been Borna. It didn't have his hair, or his warm smiling lips, or the skin, in fact. The thing in front of her was just a skeleton with patches of meat still in place, pinkish red, eyeless, lipless, but not motionless. Boney fingers scratched over pieces of meat that still hung from him.

The body was half lying, half reclining on the ground, air whistling through the holes in the bones. It clacked and twitched but, worst of all, it spoke.

"Jelena, Jelena," the air slipping over bones shaped the words, even with the complete lack of vocal cords, just a facsimile of a spoken sound, "I need to get it off me, please get it off me. This isn't me."

"I... I..." she tried to answer, her tongue stuck to the root of her mouth. The skeleton was mostly absurd, an image from an old children's cartoon. She could imagine it dancing and singing to the Great Mouse's tune. The only thing that truly made her heart ache was the knowledge, buried deep under the chaos of thoughts—there was no fixing this. She couldn't glue the pieces back together. It was what it was.

"You should stop his misery," a sudden voice whispered in her ear and Jelena shrieked. She jumped away from the source, almost tripping over Borna's bones.

For a moment, the newcomer was some unknown woman, with a shining lantern in her arms, just a kindly-faced granny on a hike. Then it clicked. It was the woman who'd rented the house to them. Milica? Tonica? Antica? Jelena hadn't really paid attention with the introduction, and it was Tina who was arranging their stay.

Tina, who was somewhere in the canyon, calling her name. Of the four of them, the only one who didn't look drunk or out of the mind. Four... *Oh, shit, where's Elrond?*

"Your eyes, that midnight blue," the woman raised the lantern, the light piercing Jelena's tender eyes,

"I see you got the true sight from my concoction, didn't know that could happen. Interesting."

Jelena raised a hand to shield herself, be it from the light or the other woman, she wasn't sure. Fear rose in her stomach like vomit, making it hard to think, to understand.

"You can see now, can't you? The world for what it is? All the nastiness hidden below what we think is real?"

Jelena swallowed down her alarm.

"Your friend, you shouldn't leave him like that." The old woman turned, coming closer to Borna's skeleton. His soft brain was still closed in the confinement of the skull.

"Don't," Jelena warned, or at least tried. She couldn't actually get her mouth to cooperate. Couldn't move away, couldn't close her eyes. Frozen to a point, too afraid and dazed to do anything.

"You know, if only you drank my gift when you were supposed to. Didn't I say it was for your welcome and that you should toast it before coming to the town? I had to send people after you to make sure we would not lose you... Well, no matter, I mean, it would've hurt you less, we would've taken care of you, but what's done is done." The woman—Ankica?—put the lamp down, and took Borna's skull in her hands. She stroked it like petting a cat, before crushing it hard on the ground. Jelena's gasp mingled with another crackling sound, because the woman continued to bash the skull down, until it was in fragments, opening up a hole for the brain.

Jelena turned away from the sight, hating herself for being so weak, such a coward to do anything for her friend, try helping him instead of just running away. The woman's laugh echoed behind her back, while the whole time the wooden horn of *sopile*—she finally recognized the sound—still played. She almost forgot about it, the music blending with the background to the point where it was as normal as the trees and the river, a part of the scenery her brain just didn't register anymore.

There was no sense in the direction she was going now, just running through the dark, the song coming for all sides, wherever she turned. Her phone's torch light was too small, too insignificant to help her get out of the canyon, far away from the woman that must've poisoned them, from Tina who had probably betrayed them.

A light appeared through the darkness, shining between trees, calling to her. She went toward the twinkling sight, wanting to get away from the dark, from shadows hiding dead friends. Bursting into the glow, she flinched, her eyes trying to shut it away. With her vision clearing, she saw that the source of light was a pair of oil torches people sometimes used in summer for the aesthetic, which were flanking the entrance of a gaping hole at the bottom of the cliff from both sides of the river.

Pazin's cave, her brain helpfully noted where she was, even though it was the first time she was seeing it from the ground level. For all the years they've visited Istrakon, she only ever saw their famous cave as an ugly wound from the hill above, the one where the castle still stood. Like some giant had pierced the rock with a sword, leaving behind a ragged wound. Jelena had never actually hiked down, or tried to get inside—that was for the more adventurous sorts, spelunkers and the like.

But it wasn't the cave nor the garden torches which made her halt in the steps. Nor was it the vague shape of a human player, blowing in the sopile at the cave's entrance, on the giant rock above her. Nor people in capes, as some cheap larpers, slowly closing in on her from the dark woods around her. No, what stole her attention completely was Elrond.

Jakov.

Her knees gave out and she fell on the ground.

His head was split open in the middle, blood pouring down, soaking the river-damp ground. He was still standing, still alive, the cranium halves hanging on by the threads of his neck, his hand touching one half like he couldn't understand what was happening. While another head was growing out of a hole inside the old one. The mangled snout was spitting ichor, the black pulsing orbs were eyes, and half formed ears twitched in the air, catching sound. Was it a dog's head? A sheep? A goat?

It was like something out of a formaldehyde-filled jar, where they stuck dead animals who never got a chance to develop.

Elrond's arm reached towards her, but his new animal head was heaving, leaking bile and blood. One of the cloaked figures came behind him and stabbed him in his guts with a silvery curved knife.

Jelena's scream deafened the shrill notes of the music, drowning it out with her own despair. This was a nightmare she couldn't wake up from. She let it all out, until there was no more air in her lungs, leaving behind only her sobs.

"What is the matter?" someone said, but she didn't care. Music started again, like nothing had happened, and she put her arms over her ears trying to muffle it.

Silence it.

"A botched transformation."

"Figures. The other one didn't get far either. He managed to get rid of his human form, but nothing replaced it."

Jelena's tears could drown her, snot and salt getting inside her mouth. She draped herself with her arms, protectively. *This can't be happening, this isn't real.*

"Why, why, why, why," she mumbled, over and over again. Borna's smile flashed in her mind, always the charming fool. His laugh a soothing timbre. Elrond's enthusiasm while he was explaining something, or his flushed face in the middle of a heated discussion over whether Jon Snow's ADWD arc made any sense or not. Even Tina, with her flannels and her compound bow, proudly cultivating the image of a prepper while teaching arts to elementary school children.

"I'm sorry, this has nothing to do with you," a voice above her said. She raised her eyes towards the speaker. The woman—Milkica?—was looking down on Jelena. Her eyes were suspiciously full of regret, and Jelena couldn't stomach them. It was her who'd given them the strange alcohol in the first place. This was all her fault. She shouldn't be standing there with a moping face, her ashen hair collected in the ponytail hanging over one shoulder.

Just like a part of her friend's face had been hanging just minutes before. He was now thrown on the ground, a part of him in the river, blood muddying the clear water.

"But we need to do this. You see, everything is wrong these days, these years. Seasons aren't changing the way they should, malicious revenants cling to our homes, and the dead are..." The woman stopped in the mid-sentence, watching somewhere over kneeling Jelena's head. "Where were *you*?" The old woman sounded part angry, part indignant, part relieved, reminding Jelena of her own mother when Jelena would do something to disappoint her. She turned around to see who the woman had been talking to, a part of her bitterly knowing who it was.

That part of her was wrong.

Jelena blinked, and started laughing hysterically. It made the tears fall even harder, making her almost choke on her own spit.

The cosplayer with a bull's mask stood there with his arms crossed on his chest.

"We found him at that festival." One of the cloaked men, who was standing right behind the cosplayer, said.

"Oh for... what have I told you about going out in public?" the woman berated the bull-man.

"That's okay, they thought he was one of the people in masks," the same man replied, and the bull snorted. Jelena's brain caught the implication of that.

"He's not... that's not... that's not a mask?" she whimpered, asking the Airbnb woman who was obviously in charge. The *sopile* suddenly stopped their dramatic play, leaving them all in a blissful silence.

The old woman sighed, tiredness overcoming her features, making her look frail, worn out. "That is my son. The last krsnik of Istria. Not that he can do anything a krsnik does." She shrugged, letting her arms fall uselessly at her side.

"What?" It was the most incredulous, most preposterous thing Jelena had heard so far, and she'd witnessed her friend alive only as a skeleton with a brain. She looked at the man they'd mistaken for a cosplayer again—this time recognizing the intelligence in his eyes, the frown in the snout, even the way he cocked his head. His horns reflected the shiny dance of the flames. How could've they ever mistaken this for a mask? Seeing it now, it was obviously real.

"I know, I know. How far have we fallen. Instead of shapeshifting, he's stuck in this halfway form. Not man, not boshkarin." The woman's voice was laced in sadness. It set a small flame of anger in Jelena.

"What does that have to do with us? Why did you do this to us?"

"We?" the woman asked incredulously. "We've done nothing to you. You all drank willingly. If you'd drank in the house upon coming here, we would've had you under control. It would've been painless." A strong urge to take the rock from the river and bash the woman's head with it surged through Jelena, making her shake hard in rage. "I mean, you would've still died. Someone has to. But it would've been a bit less traumatizing."

"I'm confused," Jelena bitterly spat and turned towards the bull-man again. "Aren't krsniks supposed to be good?" She wasn't well versed in this sort of folklore, but the long tradition of coming to Istrakon meant she'd learned a few things about legendary Istria's fighters against evil. Krsniks were supposed to heal people, help with the weather, keep them safe from the doings of the malicious shtrigas. The problem with this one wasn't that he was just stuck in between human and animal form the krsniks could take. It was also his apparent participation in the butchering of her friends. "Why are you just standing there? Letting us get slaughtered? You should help us!" *Help me*, she suddenly realized. There was no one left but her, if Tina had anything to do with this.

If a bull could look ashamed, this was how he would've probably looked. The man lowered his white head, showing her the tips of his horns.

"You don't understand. None of you on the wrong side of Uchka mountain do." Jelena laughed out loud at that, or it was simply the continuation of her last burst of delirium. "I know this is hard to understand for someone who forgot their roots, but we didn't. Look, this is nothing personal."

"I just saw my friends murdered in really bizarre ways, and I'm still not sure if I'm hallucinating because this can't be real. It can't. But, real or not, it's all because of you and your damn poison. So this is personal."

The woman rolled her eyes like Jelena was the problem, a difficult child she had to deal with. Some ignorant fool she had to educate.

The thought was a white-hot pain in her guts, wanting to consume her. She needed to find a way to use that anger to get free and turn it against this madwoman. To find a way to hurt her. And after that, the others, too. Jelena swallowed her despair. Behind the torches, shadowy forms lurked, hoods drown deeply over their faces, making it seem like there was nothing there. She couldn't count them, their numbers as vague as their bodies. There could've been anywhere from five to fifteen of them, given her limited sight, concealed by night and dark clothes. Light clung to the torches, not strong enough to brighten the canyon.

There was also the small matter of the fact that she

couldn't trust her own senses. *This is it, isn't it? My end. Why couldn't I be a final girl?*

"What are you going to do to me?" she asked, deflated, coming to terms that this was the end of her road.

The woman crouched before her, with the same kind look she had upon welcoming them in her home. Jelena had a hard time resisting spitting in her face.

"I really am sorry. If one of your men had managed to complete a transformation, I wouldn't have had to do anything. You see, the problem is, for centuries we had the krsniks, who made sure that malevolent spirits couldn't take hold of our lands. But now, we only have my son, who can barely say *moo*, much less protect anyone." Harsh. An evil lady showing no respect to her kid just because of his perceived failings; what else was new? "No new children are born with a placenta around their bodies to give them powers, so we're trying to... make our own krsniks. We still didn't get the potion right, and I'm afraid, until the time we do, we'll need to use *other* sorts of protection."

There was movement around them, slow but steady. The covered cultist—because what else should she call them—approached them on light feet, the dark tide closing in on Jelena's kneeling form.

"Mirko, please resume!" the woman shouted in the direction of the cave.

The shrill sound of the *sopile* which had followed Jelena into the canyon came back, a wail of wood pierced with holes. A ballad for her death.

"Unfortunately, where men fail, women need to step up."

For a moment, laughter almost bubbled up in

Jelena's throat. This group may be a creepy murder cult, but at least they weren't transphobes. She felt a sliver of vindication at that moment, but it was mostly crushed under the weight of how her friends had ended and that realization that, apparently, she would now die too.

"Every winter, evil comes to our home to plague us. We need to get rid of it properly. And for that, I'm afraid, we'll need your sacrifice." There was no mercy in the woman's voice. It was just a matter of fact, something that had to be done. "I can assure you, we are very grateful for that. You have our thanks."

At that point, Jelena couldn't control herself anymore and she spat in the woman's face. "Fuck you!" she screamed at the same time as hands descended on her, grabbing her. A strong pair caught her in an iron hold, lifting her from the ground. A person forced some sort of cloth in her mouth, blocking the air and her shouts. She gagged, the fabric rough on her tongue, tasting of salt.

Her upper body completely useless, she thrashed her legs, putting all the strength she had into it, trying to kick some murdering bastards in their heads, maybe even cripple someone before her untimely death. If she had to die as some sort of maiden sacrifice, at least she wanted to take at least one cultist with her. She even managed to bring one person to the ground, her feet reverberating with the strength of connecting with someone's cheek.

"Restrain her and let's move!" The woman's voice was clear even with the *sopile's* loud lamentations. It was just her luck to die while the most obnoxious music played in the background. Just like it had been her luck that the last krsnik of Istria wasn't some good guy, but a brute who was now lifting her over his back like she was nothing but a bag of potatoes, while others were binding her legs and arms. At least he didn't impale her on his horns, although who knew what they plan on doing to her. Maybe it would be better if he gutted her there and then. A completely unwelcomed memory resurfaced in her mind, that movie where evil villagers killed some young dude by strapping him on a desk and slowly drilling into his head. *Please don't let it be slow. Please don't let it be agonizing.*

Her vision swam with the bull-man's steps, the ground under her slipping from view, while they walked towards the cave. From the light, into the darkness. Maybe they'll just slit her throat. *Oh god, please let it be quick and without humiliation.* She cried in anguish. There was no way for it to be slow. It hadn't been for Borna, who'd painstakingly stripped away his body, nor for Jakov, whose head had burst like a ripe fruit, only for a new growth to rise from it. How much could that hurt? She couldn't comprehend it, but a terrifying thought, that soon she'll understand just how much pain her body could endure, burrowed in her heart and brain.

A growl joined in their procession, an angry, hungry sound vibrating in Jelena's chest. Her captor stopped, his body taut. His grip on her was so strong she feared he would crush her to death.

"What the fuck?" she heard someone say, a commotion outside her field of vision. The *sopile* ceased their incessant wailing for the second time. It wasn't silence, though, that replaced the noise. It couldn't have been, with the inhuman snarling which sounded like an earthquake stuck in the lungs of a beast.

"We're too late," Jelena recognized the woman's voice. "Oh, gods have mercy on us, we're too late." Jelena grimly smiled through her cloth. Her captors' fear was like the smell of fresh tangerines during cold autumn nights. Until: "Just slice her throat, forget the rituals."

The pain in her back exploded when she was unceremoniously dropped to the ground. A flurry of motions happened, all at the same time. The white-hot pain seared in her spine. The blurry head of a bovine swayed above her, huge and dense, crowned with pointed horns. Like an aura of death.

Please don't, she wanted to mumble, but no sound escaped from the dirty cloth. She tried to move, but her legs were tingling in a strange way, uncooperating, still bound just like her arms. At least they'd bound them in front of her, not behind, so she raised her hands in instinct, like she could stop the horns from gutting her just with her bare arms.

Screams ruptured the night, the blood churning howls of someone who was on the brink of death, unable to do a thing to stop it. People's shouts joined in the commotion, various commands spoken at the same time. Jelena couldn't even bother to try and understand with the ringing in her ears and the panic overcoming all of her senses.

The krsnik's body was still tense, his muscles straining under modern clothes which definitely didn't fit his image, now that she knew what he truly was.

"Leave her, I'll take care of her, just go deal with that thing!" The krsnik's mother entered Jelena's field of vision, an almost dismembered face floating in the air. Pointing the bullhead to some direction, probably where the worst of the screams could be heard.

The krsnik lowered his head and she begged him with her eyes. *Please. You're supposed to be the good guy!*

It was pointless. He untangled the bullwhip from his waist. Then the bull's head turned away from her, striking the air with the whip and joining in the chaos out there, while his mother came back, carrying a silver knife, the blade glittering in the light of the open flames. The adrenaline kicked in, Jelena's body twitching in an attempt to get free, an image of a turtle lying on its shell, trying to turn back upright.

The old woman straddled her, completely focused, while the screams and sounds of fighting continued to grow in the background. Splashes of something hitting the river, wet squishy sounds only human flesh could make when crushed, wails of curses and begging. The flames from a torch outlined the other woman, bathing her in red. Jelena would not give in that easily.

Scraping up all of her strength, she bucked under the woman, making her lose her balance. Her hands were still bound in front of her, but only to each other, so she used them as the boulder to hit, with all the might she could muster, at the woman's groin. The woman groaned, losing focus and strength, so Jelena managed to overturn them both with the full length of her body. Her spine screamed in agony, black dots exploding over her vision, like falling snow. Even so, she couldn't let herself fall into unconsciousness, not when that meant she would never wake again.

The knife fell from her attacker's hand, and both of them furiously tried to see how to get to it. Jelena couldn't straddle the woman in turn, too frail, bound, and awkward like a whale on dry land, so she tried to get on her knees, looking for any kind of weapon. A dismembered human leg, with a Doc Martens boot still firmly on the foot, landed near her hands. She took it clumsily, just in time, as the other woman's arm closed on the knife. Kneeling on the rough ground, feeling like a fiery hand was clutching her spine, grounding it into powder while she was still alive, Jelena screamed a battle cry through the cloth in her mouth and struck the woman's cheek with the boot part of the leg in her arms. Her captor lost the knife again, raising her elbow to protect herself from the blows. Jelena didn't care, she continued raining blows upon the woman's head.

The heel landed on the temple, hitting it with a sick crunching sound. For Borna's scratchy fingers, wearing himself to the bone.

She hit again, the boot connecting with the forehead in a loud crack, for Jakov's broken head.

More and more wounds opened under the blows, blood pouring thick from the holes, white, fractured bone particles and rosy brain matter spilling out with the hits, splattering all over Jelena. Getting in her eyes, in her nostrils, in her hair. She inhaled her would-be killer with each breath, minuscule drops of blood and fragments of bone traveling through her nose down to her throat.

Jelena didn't stop. Only when the crushed head under her was an unrecognizable soup of anatomical parts, did she finally let the bloody leg, with chunks of brain stuck on the heel, fall on the ground.

Wheezing from weariness and pain, she dragged the cloth out of her mouth, her hands still bound together. At least she could breathe again, inhaling in big gasps. She was completely drenched in fatigue and sweat, her whole body on fire. Afraid of what was waiting for her outside her own bubble of light, where the screams were slowly decreasing in strength, she knew full well she couldn't fight off anyone stronger than the old woman she'd wrestled with. Slowly, praying to the gods, to anyone who could hear her, she raised her head.

It was a complete carnage.

That was it. The only way she could explain what she was watching. The flames of the torches still illuminated the ground, now littered with dismembered body parts. Cultists gored like cows, their insides stretching from the rips in their stomachs. Butchered bodies were strewn in the river stream, the water darkening with crimson. It was more of a slaughterhouse than a battlefield, and she could envision someone picking up the discarded meat, grounding it down into the tender filling for sausages. In the middle of it all, two figures were still fighting.

Her vision was blurry, partially for the pain, partially from the night and the dancing light source. One figure was the krsnik, whom she could recognize by his white, hairy head, and the other…

The other form was much bigger, like a boulder made of muscles. The horns were similar to the krsnik's in shape but much thicker. And the head; she couldn't be sure, not under this light, but something was wrong with it. It was a bull's head, she supposed but, at the same time, it had a strange cubic shape no cattle head ever had. The hair on the snout was completely black, but she could spot a white, knotted mane on the back. Huge canines glistened in the dancing light.

Then the creature let out a roar before lowering its head, using the impressive build of its build to mow down the krsnik with sheer force. Like a mountain swatting down a fly. Jelena's memory flared with the familiarity of the move. It was simple but effective, something she saw hundreds of times at the carnival of Rijeka.

The bellmen from the Kastav area were always the last in the parade, famous for their brutal performance, the same one every year. They would use their bodies to charge at the front lines of the audience, walking in a line, shaking their hips so that the cattle bells on their belts could ring out loudly. They would walk menacingly toward other people in the crowd, lowering their heads before tackling the loose metal fence which was the only, flimsy barrier between the spectators and those in the parade. You never stood close to the line when they did their dance unless you wanted to get trampled under the bodies of the shocked onlookers who were being pushed out.

This was the exact same move the big creature used, tackling the krsnik to the ground, and that's why she was finally able to recognize it for what it was. A real, living bellman, not just a mask. Well, sans the actual bell.

The other thing she recognized were the shredded clothes still sticking to the body in places. The red plaid pattern, the dark jeans. Tears of relief and joy muddled her view and she let out a sob.

Tina's arms weren't resembling human ones anymore. They were as big as a trunk of a birch, covered in black fur, drenched with blood. She caught the horns of the krsnik, lying on the ground, between her gigantic palms, and started to stretch them outwards. The bull's shriek set Jelena's jaw on edge, his pain so profound she could feel it vibrating in her own bones. The krsnik thrashed, but Tina kneeled on his chest and, with a snarl of her own and a nasty crunch, she ripped off the horns from his head.

There was no comparison for the scream that tore from the bull's mouth—high-pitched, gurgling, it clenched Jelena's insides in a compassionate knot. The krsnik's thrashing was getting slower, blood surging like a big, unobstructed stream from the twin wounds on his forehead. Tina turned over the torn-out horn in her right hand and stabbed him with it in the throat.

For a moment there was no sound. A grave silence fell on the canyon at the entrance of the great cave of Pazin. An oppressive lack of noise which followed the massacre.

Dread slowly trickled out of Jelena, as did her suspicions at Tina. A feeling that something was wrong with her friend finally dissipated, seeing her finally for what she was, in all her might. She wasn't sure what had been happening with her sight before, whatever the potion had done to her. Had she actually seen the beginnings of Tina's transformation, or was it something else? Without understanding what the cultist had done to her, she couldn't discern what was true. Jelena just knew that, whatever fuckery was induced by the thing they drank, it made her run away and mistrust her oldest friend. Well, not anymore.

Jelena sat there, her limbs still bound, a bashed in head of the woman she killed close to her hands, on the ground. Tina, on the other hand, stood among the butchered cultists' bodies.

Her monstrous form started moving towards

Jelena, and for a moment she was aware of a lot of things. Blood clinging to Tina's changed hair and clothes, skin tissue hanging from her horns. Tina's hands could beat Jelena to a bloody pulp without breaking a sweat. Or she could gut Jelena, a clean strike with a pointed horn, from one end of her abdomen to the other. Tina could do so much to her that she'd already done to the others, with enough strength to just pull out Jelena's arm from its socket and fling it away, as if it were nothing but a small rock on the shore.

The enormous body, part human, part bull, part something completely terrifying, crouched in front of Jelena, so mindful of its horns that Jelena didn't feel afraid of accidental stabbing. With clumsy moves, thanks to her thick fingers, Tina managed to untangle Jelena's bonds.

"Thanks," Jelena's voice croaked, and she went on to release her legs, while Tina sat down in front of her.

The strange calm continued, and Jelena sighed in choked happiness that her limbs were free. She wasn't even worried that her body tingled in an ominous way, too relieved to still be alive and breathing to feel pain. Tina put her gigantic head in her hands, and Jelena was pretty certain the girl was quietly sobbing.

"Hey, hey, it's okay." It wasn't. Of course, it wasn't. Their friends were dead. Jelena had almost been sacrificed. Tina's whole body had transformed into a beast.

She felt so bad for running away from her before. For not trusting her.

She leaned against Tina, embracing her in a hug, almost disappearing in her great mane. Breathing in the smell of earth, soil, and death.

"Ha! Look who's a bellman now! Not your dad, for sure! Fuck his costume, he can never be the real deal. Not like you." Jelena's shoulders shook from laughing even when it brought her nothing but searing hot pain. But her joke worked. Tina put a hand, as big as Jelena's two, over hers, and started rumbling with a deep laugh of her own.

The bellmen brought spring, and even though the season had already changed with the calendar, Jelena had a hunch that it didn't count. Not until now.

Whatever they'd just gone through, at least they hadn't been alone in it.

Embraced like this, tiredness overcame them—two women, one of which was a beast, waiting for the dawn, crying over the dead. While, above their heads, they could hear people's voices and shouts, a crowd gathering, called to the canyon with the sounds of their fighting.

She just hoped it was the geeks and not more cultists.

The Lottery

"Ooooooooj! Flare up!"

Even though she knew what was going to happen next, Augusta flinched at the sudden drum, drowning the quieter sound of the simultaneous igniting of torches. Four young women stood in a circle, each with a torch in hand. Slowly, they started coming closer to the middle, where Lana stood waiting, deathly calm as if she were carved from stone. She held an apple in her hand, meager and wrinkled but, even like that, it had still been the best they could find.

"*O, la, la, la,*" the other women vocalized, chanting in the drum's rhythm. Even though she could not hear the rain, Augusta imagined the slight murmur in the background, the drops falling on the roofs of their houses, joining in the melody down here in the cellar.

"*Oj, oj Lado, oj!*" the four girls shouted, raising the torches high above Lana's head.

"Up, up, higher!" Augusta heard someone yell, just before she breathed in the smell of burned hair. She frowned, unhappy with the fact that she couldn't see Lana anymore, crammed between four girls, under the fire from the torches. Until now, that had been the only good part of this whole evening she was forced to participate in. She'd lurked undisturbed, keeping track of Lana's every breath, every blink of her eyelashes. Now, Augusta could only see a few small details—a part of the face, a part of slightly scorched hair—and all of that between the arms and the heads of the girls pressing closer over Lana.

"La, la, la, la, oh, oh, oh," the girls sang, as close to Lana as the flames would let them. The other women, gathered in the big circle around them, joined in the song. Augusta was the only one who was standing calmly outside of it, in the background. If she were a better daughter, maybe she would've been involved, too, even standing there in the center of it all as one of the torchbearers, huddled close to Lana. Instead, she was forgotten in a dark corner of the room, as if she were some sort of a spooky specter, while it was her oldest sister who was a part of the inner circle, with a torch in her hand.

"Oj, Lado!"

A deafening scream—guttural, deep, primordial—cut through the drumming, the women's chanting, and the rain, the drizzle of which Augusta heard only in her head. This time, she didn't recoil from the sound. A second shriek accompanied the first. Then the third.

Almost shyly, a sound of an ax chopping joined in the melody.

The girls moved out of the circle. As if on some secret mark, Augusta crept closer. She inhaled deeply. The smell of burnt hair, sweat, and moisture couldn't compare with the metallic scent of blood tingling in her nostrils. Gushing crimson poured over Lana, her feet, her luscious hair, the color of wheat. She closed her eyes, shuddering lightly under the cascade of blood. Like a branch under a storm's surge. The women held three beheaded bodies in their arms until the last twitching of the dead limbs. Augusta's second sister—with a nettle stem in her hair—held a rooster. Their Aunt held an eagle. And Mother held a man.

A strong need to break through the other women in the circle to get to Lana—to lick all of the blood from her body, until her skin was clean and pure again—surged through Augusta. Nudging her to move from her spot. She licked her lips, feeling how rough and dry they were. It was madness, she knew, but she continued coming closer to the petrified girl drenched in crimson fluid. Someone's hand shot out and grabbed Augusta, stopping her. The hand was wet from blood, Augusta noticed before she even saw who was holding her. It was Aunt, her eyebrow arched in her questioning face. With a firm shake, she showed Augusta that she needed to move away. *Before your mother sees you*, Augusta imagined her Aunt saying.

Rolling her eyes, she changed her direction. Aunt had left a bloody print on Augusta's arm.

Augusta pouted, crossing her arms on her chest, waiting for the sounds of the drum, the song, and the flames to die out. Hoping that the rain will finally stop.

She squeezed the wet rag, making watered-down blood drip from it. She shook it three times before she dropped it on the floor with a dramatic sigh. Her knees were killing her, but this was the faster way to mop down the floor. Especially since she was hiding the fact that she'd accidentally broken a mop in half from her Mother. And, because they were saving up the batteries, she couldn't use the electrical cleaner. So she kneeled and rubbed with all her might, using rainwater to dilute dried-out blood, knowing fully well there was no chance to clean it all up. This must've been some sort of punishment, there was no chance of the contrary. She just wasn't sure what she'd done this time to deserve her Mother's schooling.

Augusta raised a hand in front of her. The thick rubber glove glistened. Not for the first time, she fell into the temptation to lick her fingers. Just a little, to taste it, to sate her curiosity. To learn the taste of blood, watered-down in rainwater, and the detergent which smelled of vodka and essential oils. Could she notice the difference, guess what came from the body and what didn't, or was it all too mixed up, homogeneous? Would rainwater, even diluted like this, burn her tongue?

A memory of Lana, standing there drenched in blood, like some sort of war goddess, resurfaced in her mind.

Sulking, Augusta continued to roughly rub the floor, smearing the crimson more and more, coloring the gray of the concrete with a pink of a child's dream. "Futile," she said out loud, although no one got to hear her.

"Di je, ni je, u poju je, u poju je, bere ruže," she started singing quietly so she wouldn't get bored to death. *"Bere ruže i vijole, na na ne na ni ne na."* She wasn't even sure why she'd remembered this song. This conserving of electricity is going to kill her. She couldn't use any of the devices she usually did for listening to music or watching movies while she worked on menial tasks. Just like this, she was supposed to be her own entertainment and it just wasn't cutting it.

She made exactly eleven motions with her rag—she counted, somewhere in the back of her thoughts—and, with the ending of the song, she decided she was finished. It wasn't anywhere near clean. In fact, it looked even worse than before, like someone had puked all over the floor, spreading digested raspberries. There was no way she would ever manage to clean it all up but, if anyone asked her, there was no need for that. Her opinions didn't matter, though. The only thing that mattered was what her Mother wanted. And she won't be happy with the job done.

Augusta bit her lip. Glanced at the watch under her glove. The council meeting was soon, something that not a lot of people in their village even knew was happening. She was certain that there was only one item on today's agenda. Success or, better said, the lack of one; the failure of their last ritual, given that it was still raining. Everyone was nervous, waiting for what would happen next, but until the council made an official announcement, the only thing they could do was guess. Augusta had a hunch that, whatever the council decided, it would definitely be something bad. Thankfully, she had a way to learn what the council would do, before everyone else did.

After a short contemplation, knowing fully well she could incur her Mother's rage if she got caught—or, at least, a great disappointment when her botched job got noticed—she threw the rag in the bucket and hurriedly put on her hazmat raincoat. In bright orange, she felt like a walking lighthouse. She just hoped her Mother was too busy to actually take notice of Augusta's whereabouts.

Rushing up the stairs, she climbed to the enormous metal door. The smell of feathers and manure hit her nostrils as soon as she opened it. She expected to see chickens scattered on the hay out of boredom from being locked inside, while one lonely cow gazed at the wall, and a stranger rotted in the corner, but not that there would be Lana inside, too—jumping at the sound of the opening door.

Augusta froze mid-step, surprised. Her gaze stuck to Lana, whose disheveled golden hair was like a halo while she was trying to fix her crumpled, half-unbuttoned clothes. It was only then that Augusta's eyes moved, finding, at last, Renato, who looked as confused as Augusta felt. Their hazmat raincoats were a discarded heap on the floor, and one rooster was using it as its throne. Thanks to the complete soundproofing of the basement, Augusta had stumbled upon the pair completely unprepared. Now she stood there in silence, still, unsure how to act. Were they having an actual romp in the hay because everyone was stuck inside, so they were desperate enough for privacy that the stables would do? What century was this?

But, it did follow a sort of logic. The only ones to be able to intrude on their privacy here were the chickens, a cow, and the imprisoned thief who lay in the corner—reserved usually for the calf—and that one couldn't see a thing or say a word, or bother them in any other way.

She felt the chickens watching the scene intently, judging.

"Augusta! You freaked us out. My heart almost gave out!" Lana was the first one to shake out of her reverie, putting a palm on her chest. On the soft skin visible under an unbuttoned shirt.

"We, ah... came to feed the chickens," Renato said awkwardly, for some reason blushing to the roots of his hair. That, she didn't expect. Not from him—always smiling and so full of himself, showing off his hunting prowess and biceps alike, as well as his woodland skills and alcohol drinking; taking care of does in the winter and shooting the rabbits from an awe-inspiring distance. Augusta arched her eyebrow at his statement, keeping quiet.

"Er, yes," Lana said, edging closer to him as if she were using him as a shield as if Augusta would do something to her. The thought saddened, but didn't surprise her.

"The chickens were already fed," she said, in lack of anything smart to add, but wanting to show she wasn't a danger to them. Renato fidgeted, looking like a person getting poked in the butt by a bull. He probably wanted to run away from there as fast as he could. Actually, she wasn't sure why both of them hadn't done that already.

"Doesn't matter," Augusta continued, anticipating that something really foolish will come out of her mouth next, "they're always hungry." She was right.

Lana nodded as if this conversation made sense. Her eyes were huge, unblinking. Augusta wondered whether she would've been afraid if it were anyone else to catch them, or did she react like that just to Augusta?

"You can go, I'm gonna finish here." She wasn't sure, exactly, what that meant, but both of them looked spooked, like animals caught in a trap, and that was starting to annoy her. And as if they'd been waiting for her permission, without a word they put their raincoats and masks back on, so fast it was comical to watch, and rushed from the stable, out into the rain. The rooster who'd been snuggled on the heap of their hazmats angrily watched after them, ousted from his place, fluttering his wings as if he were cursing after them.

"They're really rude, aren't they?" she asked him. He cockadoddled in agreement. "Maybe he should get a small cold, nothing bad. Tonsillitis, mayhaps," she continued, imagining that she could see Renato through the wall. The cow mooed from her position. "I was just joking," she calmly said to the animals around her. She checked the man who still lay there in silence, hidden behind a short door, all broken bones and dried out. He didn't look like someone who might try to run away, even if they hadn't paralyzed him. He won't endure long, but that wasn't her problem. It did remind her of her quest, though. The council had already gathered at this point, surely.

She stopped in front of the door and drew the hood of her raincoat over her head, checking if it was properly closed. Unlike Lana and Renato, who'd come here under full protection, Augusta didn't have a mask, but she did have goggles, which hung on a rack. She wouldn't be in the open for too long, but it was still smart to protect her eyes. Even when the wind wasn't blowing, the raindrops got everywhere.

Only when she was satisfied that her skin was properly protected, did she open the door and ran towards the main house.

Dropping away everything wet in the disinfection box at the main door, she rushed to the attic and almost knocked into her Aunt. Her long brown hair had been firmly set in a slick bun, which is why she looked much stricter than she usually was. Augusta noted that she wore a clean, pressed white blouse with equally straight and smooth slacks, which was so impractical for their situation that even if Augusta hadn't known that the council was planning to meet, this whole getup would've been a pretty obvious hint.

"Careful, where's the rush?" Aunt asked her, catching Augusta by the arm again. She smiled slightly, but couldn't hide the worry under her discerning green eyes.

"In the kitchen," Augusta answered, pushing her guilt from lying under her own smile. "I was planning to help." That she'd said something completely unconvincing, she only became aware of after finishing her sentence. The Aunt, of course, watched her with arched eyebrows.

"Mhm. Now the truth. Or don't tell me, maybe it's better for me not to know."

Augusta felt even worse than before. Her cheeks burned in shame, reminding her of Renato. That, in turn, just irritated her further.

So she shrugged, watching her Aunt with the confidence of someone who surely spoke the truth, and nothing but the truth. "Alright, I'm hungry and too impatient to wait for dinner. I was planning to beg or, you know, give them a stinky eye, until the kitchen staff relented and gave me something for a bite. Please, don't tell mom; you know she doesn't like it when we do that. Plus—" she got a sudden burst of inspiration "—I would really like to help, but only if they let me. It's not my fault everyone here is full of prejudice."

That she'd gone too far with the last comment, she realized as soon as she saw her Aunt's pitiful look. Augusta didn't want to play the card that no one had any faith in her; that, in the eyes of the others, she was always to blame for everything, from the common cold to the tumors. Now her Aunt was feeling bad, the only person in the whole village who didn't deserve to.

"I'm sorry, that sounded too harsh, it was meant to

be a joke," Augusta said in the end, watching her feet.

The silence lasted for three minutes, only to be broken by her Aunt's loud sigh. "I will not snitch on you to your mom. I'm sure there's enough food. Agi..." Aunt put her arm on Augusta's shoulder. "I would like to hang out with you a little longer, but I need to go. They're waiting for me." She emphasized the plural, but Augusta still heard the unspoken *your mother is waiting*. Relieved that she got away with her lie, she said goodbye to Aunt and continued towards the kitchen.

At least that part had been true. While passing through the main hall, she almost got hit in the head because, out of boredom, some kids had managed to find a ball to play dodgeball with. Shyly, they greeted her while the grownups, sitting with books or talking under the energy-saving bulbs, suspiciously stared at her. Because of the weather, and the general conservation of electricity in the whole village, there were even more people than usual in her home. It was, after all, the biggest and safest house, which meant that the crowd that usually came to them had doubled, up to the point it felt, for Augusta, like the whole village was now stuck in one building.

After the great hall, she strode into the vast kitchen, where a group of women was standing over the cheese reel, with protective goggles and masks over their mouths. All five heads looked in her direction, frowning.

"What are you doing here? Do you want larvae in your eye?" one of them asked, a cousin who lived with them.

"I'm just passing through. Is there anything to nibble on?"

"We can't give away anything before dinner, don't act so childish," her cousin continued. "Go away and stop bothering us."

Augusta shrugged. "Maybe there'll be something in the attic," she said to the glowering women. Her cousin rolled her eyes but otherwise didn't dare to forbid her to pass.

None of them did. Throwing a final glance at the cooks, who were checking whether the cheese was safe for dinner, she closed the doors behind her, reminding herself that she shouldn't eat the cheese tonight. Chewing the live larvae took forever.

The smells of the stagnant attic air and the sausages drying on the hooks greeted her. There was more food, of course, stored on the shelves; various jams, flour, spices, and pickled vegetables. The attic stretched through the whole length of the building and, except for the food, it was littered with old furniture, broken appliances, and documents. Quietly, gracefully, she managed to squeeze through the junk and come to the other end of the room, where she knelt by the opening of the old chimney, out of use for ages, but which apparently hadn't been closed well enough, which is the way it conducted sound from the room below. Something which Augusta had learned by complete accident once, doing some of the unnecessary chores her Mother gave her.

"Rijeka is completely cut off," she heard one of the older women say. "No one can get in or out of town, until the rain calms down."

"Down there, it's both rain and wind. With bora that strong, I wouldn't be surprised if they had Chemprotex glued to their skin perpetually," said Augusta's Mother, impatiently.

"I don't even want to try to imagine how it is in Senj," the third voice piped in, an old woman Augusta didn't like too much, mostly because she was the one who'd convinced the others that Sardinian people had good taste where cheese was concerned, but not just because of that.

"Maybe it will calm down. Give it some time and…" This time, it was Aunt, quieter than the rest, which is why Augusta couldn't follow the rest of the sentence.

"Oh please, you're so naive. If the ritual had worked, Lada would've already granted us our wish. She's ignoring us, just like the goddess Vesna before her. We need to make peace with the fact that the Gods haveleft us to handle this ourselves," Mother's voice thundered in Augusta's ears. "They are probably brawling again, so they don't have time for us mortals."

"Maybe we've done something wrong, maybe…" the fourth voice joined in, but left the sentence hanging in the air, as if the speaker wasn't sure how to finish her thought.

"Maybe nothing. It's still raining," Mother cut the discussion short. "Eugenija, what are our battery levels like?" she asked her sister.

"Good, for now. Panels are still generating electricity, although the productivity lowered when—"

"Didn't we get the hybrid ones so that we could get energy from the rain, too?" one of the other women interrupted Augusta's Aunt.

"They were never meant to compensate for all of the energy we could get from the sunlight. Only to reduce the loss, which would be even greater if we didn't have the hybrids. In any case, that's not what worries me. The fact is, we don't know how long the solar cells can hold in this rain until the inevitable damage occurs. Moreover, we can kiss our orchard and outside garden goodbye. There's no way the food will be edible after this, or that anything new will even grow there. Thereat, when we take into account the air quality and the fact that the filters also run on electricity, who knows—" She suddenly stopped. Augusta wasn't sure if her Aunt was talking quieter again, or if something had cut her off, which Augusta couldn't see.

"So, what now?" the fifth voice asked.

Dead silence. She could imagine Mother looking over the others with a disappointed look, which probably motivated them to figure out a solution for their problems more than any sickness, famine, death or long-term loss of the internet. Out of everything, Augusta was worrying about the latter the most.

"What about that sharkanj that lives in the vicinity?" one of the women asked. "In any other situation, I would propose we went and begged Trsat's dragon, but with the current situation in Rijeka, I'm not sure that would be the smartest course of action, even if we could get into the town."

"Forget it, *he* would not help us," Augusta's Mother answered, firmly.

"I know he doesn't... like us, but when his grandmother was alive, guarding her river, we were always able to reach an agreement with her."

"But she's gone now. Besides, the kid told us to fuck off a few times before; told us he didn't need us and to stop bothering him." Mother was getting angrier, a curse slipping from her usually proper self. Obviously, she wasn't happy with the direction of the discussion.

"Plus, we have no idea if he would be *able* to help us," Aunt jumped in. "Don't you go to his kind when you *want* the storm? Not the other way around?"

"They say the sharkanj can drink the whole river, and what is rain, if not vertical water? The one who can bring the rain can probably get rid of it, too. I think we shouldn't ignore this possibility."

"But even if we wanted to, how could we coax him into helping us?"

For a few minutes, there was silence again, and then Mother's voice flew up the chimney, heavy and cold: "The old way." Augusta felt chills go down her body, knowing she won't like whatever was coming next. "Snakes like him are similar to dragons. They are so closely related that some people view them as river dragons. For the magic, that's enough. We offer him a sacrifice, as we would to a normal dragon. That way, bound by magic and tradition like all of us, he would not be able to refuse us."

"Do you think that the thief will be pleasing enough? He's a little broken and half dead, not much of a sacrifice," the woman Augusta disliked the most in the council, spoke with the most sense right now, it would appear.

"She's not thinking of him." Aunt's voice was cold, but not out of anger, but because of a hidden terror that Augusta had no problem recognizing.

"That offering wouldn't be a real sacrifice. We're going to keep the stranger for ourselves. And to the sharkanj, we will bring one of us."

"You would sacrifice one of our girls." Aunt sounded upset, but not surprised. The others started speaking at the same time, their words blending in so Augusta couldn't understand them.

"As it was once done," her Mother answered a question Augusta hadn't heard, loud and clear. "We will hold the lottery. That way will be the most fair."

"Mira, you're speaking nonsense." Aunt was the only one that dared to go against her, the others getting silent. "We can just wait for the weather to calm down, I'm sure it won't rain forever. It's better then to make a sacrifice to someone who is not really a dragon, nor the best choice for the job we will ask of him."

"You can wait, but I refuse to be passive, especially when there are things that we could do to stop this. Midsummer is soon. You know what the magical power we can harvest from the sun that day. And you would want us to, what, lose it to the rain? Everything else we've tried has failed. I don't know what to do anymore. And you?"

"I know I would surely *not* sacrifice one of our children. What is wrong with you, Gods almighty? This is not some stranger stumbling onto our territory, or the gang of brigands, or monsters from the dark. These are our daughters, our flesh and blood, every single one of them."

A deafening silence accompanied her words. Augusta hugged her knees. She hoped someone else would oppose her Mother and take her Aunt's side. But, no matter how long she waited, that didn't happen. Cowards, every single one of them.

"So, the lottery," her Mother said.

"We're going to write all the women's names, but can we do men's, too?" someone asked.

"It was always women and girls, it's better to stick to the good old recipe," Mother said, as if they were talking about making dumplings with plums. "Of course, no younger than twelve and no older than forty. We will, also, exempt some names, secretly, of course," Mother continued.

"Of course," Aunt said sarcastically, her voice full of venom. Augusta was pretty sure that, after this, there would be a great row between the two sisters, but her Aunt wouldn't lose her cool now, not before others.

"I can see the way you're looking at me, but you know yourself that some are more useful to our community than the rest. Eugenija, don't you dare roll your eyes at me. What would we do if we drew Antea's name out, who would heal us without her powers then? Do you remember the smallpox? Or what if we drew your name? Or Minea's," Mother named one of the councilwomen's granddaughters, probably looking right at the woman in question. "Or anyone else whose abilities and power are necessary for our village to stay safe? We can't handicap ourselves like that."

"And who will choose which names go, and which don't, into the lottery? Don't say *the council*, because we both know that, in the end, your word will have the most power..."

Augusta stood up slowly and, as quietly as she got there, so she went away. If she'd stayed any longer, the cooks might become suspicious, and she'd already heard everything she had to. She didn't need, or want, to hear the rest. Especially, she didn't want to know who was indispensable to the village, apparently, and who was the waste.

Her appetite lost, she returned to the stable, and continued to rub away at the bloody floor.

They were all dressed in white woolen dresses, as the old way demanded, apparently. The fabric was scratchy and warm, making it harder to breathe in an already nauseating situation. The whole village, or, at least, the most of it, grudgingly pressed together in the great hall. Augusta could hear the drizzling of the rain, the reason for their gloomy gathering. The girls had been singled out in front of the small stage, gathered closely, with fearful eyes. Augusta stood alongside them, her thoughts a mess, as she observed it all.

It wasn't just the clothes that they'd had to choose carefully—they all wore formal braids, except for those who kept their hair short, and each of them wore flower crowns on their heads. Most of it was fake, of course, mostly sunflowers which had been destroyed in the fields; then there were the imitations of red roses and a rare poppy or two. Augusta's sisters wore real flowers, from the small greenhouse—purple irises, woven with their meaty green leaves into complicated, luscious buns. Augusta had also utilized what grew in the greenhouse, but she chose rosemary with blossoming flowers, pinning the herb over her ears. Mother had been surprised when she saw her a few hours earlier, while they were getting ready for the ceremony.

"What? I'm also your daughter; just because I'm not a priestess, it doesn't mean I don't know symbolism," Augusta had told her. Mother didn't have anything to say to that. She had just continued watching her with a predatory gaze. Augusta's sisters had been watching them, confused.

"Rosemary is connected to the sun. And to death," Augusta had explained to them, drawing a bitter satisfaction from knowing something they did not. Ultimately, though, she knew it would have no effect on her Mother. "So, two birds, one stone." Saying that, she had started laughing loudly, alarming her sisters and irritating their Mother.

In the present, Augusta was watching how her oldest sister Antea hugged her wife with one hand, and their daughter with the other—the only one who wasn't a part of the sacrificial group, too young for her name to be written into the lottery. Antea stood in a fitful fear, as if there were any chance that her name, or the name of her loved one, might be in the raffle drum. As if their Mother would ever allow it. Augusta knew Antea was safe, but she didn't know who else. She let her gaze roam over the others. Finding Lana in the middle of her friends, holding on to each other tightly with closed eyes and quiet singing or, maybe, a prayer. Was her name inside? A touch of panic bit Augusta in the chest, thinking that the drum could spin and spit out Lana's name.

The silence was sudden and surprising, given the number of mouths stuck together in the hall. The council climbed up on stage one by one. Augusta's Mother was in the center, carrying the huge, homemade raffle drum with ease. Through Mother's black, old ceremonial dress, Augusta could glimpse the tense muscles and bull-strong shoulders. The other women followed her in a procession, also in black, except for Aunt, who strode onto the stage in a dark red suit, the only one to wear color. She looked like a smear of blood, with an angry face she didn't even try to hide. She'd cut her long brown hair, completely shaving it off. Augusta assumed Mother had raged mad when she saw her. In the last few days, their relationship had been filled with a perpetual string of fights.

Augusta's Mother started talking, everyone

hanging intently on her every word. Even if she wanted to bother with listening, Augusta couldn't hear her. There was a sort of a white noise humming in her ears, as if she were floating on the surface of the sea, which is why her eyes kept wandering around the room. Over Aunt's shaved head, the whiteness engulfing Augusta, the drum that would decide who lives and who would give their life to stop the rain. Who was the worthiest one among them?

That last thought had spun in her mind ever since she'd refused to listen to the end of that discussion, back in the attic. The number of the pieces of paper had to stay the same as the number of women and girls, forced into small, numbered balls her Mother had shown to the gathered people, but Augusta knew all of them weren't written in. There would be no blank pieces, because opening one with no name that would mean a certain mutiny. So, some had to have been written multiple times. Was her name there twice, once for her and once in Antea's place? Or Lana's? Suddenly, a thought struck her, burning her whole body as if someone had thrown her out in the rain naked.

What if all of the names in the drum were actually hers?

Augusta.

Augusta.

On each paper, just that—Augusta.

The drum stopped and the collective, angsty inhale broke through her heavy musings. When had they spun it? It didn't matter. Her Mother took the ball from the table. Lana's face was scrunched, ready to start crying, while her look constantly fled to Renato, there near the end of the hall, like she was waiting for him to deliver her from evil. The ball opened, and everyone could see a slip of paper between Mother's fingers.

"WAIT!" Augusta's voice rang through the whole length of hall, loud and forceful, the one person no one could ignore. Mother stopped, with the paper opened so only she could see what was written, without a comment. She was watching Augusta thoroughly, as if she could see under her white dress and the rosemary, under the chest and skin, blood and meat, all the way to the bone.

Augusta approached the stage, in no rush, counting every step, knowing all the eyes were fixed on her. Let them watch. Let them fear. No one dared to say a thing to her. Her eyes were locked onto Mother's gaze, herAunt trying to signal something to her at the periphery.

"There's no need for this," Augusta said loudly, so everyone could hear.

She climbed onto the stage and took the paper from Mother's hands. Mother let her, completely numb in surprise, although it was hard to say with her unchanging, eagle eyes.

Still, Augusta knew.

She closed down the paper slip without even seeing what was written there in calligraphy.

"As the third daughter of the high priestess, my sacrifice should suffice," she proclaimed to the audience, which looked like they'd forgotten how to breathe. In the background, she could hear her Aunt curse. "There's no need to draw anyone else out."

"I know I'm not a priestess," she added quietly, so only her Mother could hear, "but I know how symbolism works. You couldn't have a better candidate."

A deafening silence was the only thing left after her stunt, covering the hall as a heavy, velvety coverlet. Then her Mother nodded, and the others collectively exhaled.

"Your sacrifice is accepted, dear child," Mother's voice sealed her choice. The sounds of a frenzied joy, happiness and surprise erupted in the hall.

Augusta left the crumpled paper in Mother's hand, not even wanting to see who had been drawn out. She didn't need to know. Turning toward the others, she carefully watched their reactions. Her oldest sister, Antea, cried, but Augusta couldn't be sure whether it was on her behalf, or out of happiness that her wife and she had been spared. Augusta didn't have time to contemplate it. Her other sister tried to hide the relief which was shining unconcealed on so many faces. Still, the group of women in the first row caught Augusta in their arms and pulled her over to themselves, their faces radiating, full of gratitude. Lana was among them, too, who even went so far to hug Augusta, without fear.

"Thank you," she whispered in Augusta's ear, with her sing-song voice, "thank you."

Augusta grinned, ear to ear. Not a moment too soon, Lana was out of her hands, before she could reply. In that moment, the group detached from her, like a school of fish before a predator. She fully expected to turn and see Mother behind her back, but it was actually her Aunt standing there, shivering from rage. Nevertheless, she embraced Augusta in an iron-tight hug and whispered, so only Augusta could hear her: "You foolish, stubborn brat. Why couldn't you stay silent?"

"Someone must go, Auntie. Better me than someone else." *Someone better than me*, she wanted to add, but didn't. Aunt let her out of her hands reluctantly, and kissed her on the forehead.

"This, I would not forgive her, ever." There wasn't any need to explain who she'd meant.

Speaking of the devil, as soon as she mentioned her sister, Augusta's Mother also broke through the gathered crowd. She put her hand on Augusta's shoulder and spoke—loudly, for everyone's benefit.

"You did a great thing for our community, today. We are all very proud." Someone repeated after her, and soon people started shouting how proud they all were. Mother engulfed her with one arm and, like that, they went towards Augusta's room.

Walking, Augusta saw Renato kissing the tears of joy from Lana's face. Even now, in Augusta's big moment, Lana still didn't care for her in the slightest. Only then, watching the lovers locked in kiss, did it finally dawn on Augusta what she had done.

She remembered her Aunt's comment. She indeed was a foolish girl.

Ignoring Lana and Renato, and the whole world with them, she looked straight in front of her.

No one could take away the fact that, in that moment, she was the most important and most welcomed person in the village. Their saviour, instead of their undoing.

And they were preparing her for the snake, not a *real* dragon. How scary could that really be?

They sent her with an escort—allegedly, so she wouldn't be alone on this tragic path, but she had a suspicion it was because they wanted to be sure she would not change her mind and run. This way, they could keep an eye on her. Mother had also claimed it was for her protection, because you never could be sure with all the evils lurking in the forest, outside the protection from her village. Augusta was fully aware that she could handle any sort of trouble, but they all had to act like she was some powerless maiden for the ritual to work flawlessly. She'd ended up saying nothing at that. In fact, what was truly missing was the whole procession which should've followed her, but couldn't, thanks to the rain. This is why, behind Augusta, only two women—of the village guards—walked, hidden under layers of protective clothes and gear.

Augusta didn't get the mask, so her face could stay uncovered. Fortunately, they'd decided that she should be able to see where she walked, so they let her wear goggles. Regardless of the fact that she wore a hazmat raincoat and thick rubber boots, she could still feel the scorching warmth of the rain and its pungent smell, which made her gag. They were in luck, though, that it wasn't pouring. It would've made the trek through the dusky forest even slower.

She'd hoped that they would've used the car for some of the short journey, at least for the part that was still passable, but Mother refused. Because of the need to conserve electricity, apparently. So they had to brave the dark, wet forest dripping with toxic rain on foot, hoping they weren't going to stumble upon some of the undesirables. Those who'd been kicked out of the towns, who were on the run or who wanted to, simply, spread murder and chaos.

The sharkanj lived close by but, to Augusta, it felt like they were walking the whole day. Or, maybe, a whole eternity. Her escorts were silent, ignoring every attempt at a conversation Augusta had made. When she started singing, they stopped her, harshly. After that, Augusta closed her mouth and continued to hum.

She'd played a whole album of Icelandic post-rock in her head, and had just started on the ballads, when they finally came upon the swelled-up river. In the dusk of the night, it appeared black. Under the lights of their lamps, it seemed so dark green it gave an appearance of pumpkin seed oil. One of the women pulled Augusta towards the river, carefully, showing her to the water while staying behind, herself. Knowing what was expected from her, Augusta took off her glove and offered her hand to the woman, palm up. The raindrops hit her skin, leaving a piercing hot trail, burning more intensely with time. Still, she said nothing, and waited for the guard to do her thing with a cool face, betraying nothing of her hurt.

The guard drew out the ancient-looking knife, with a handle carved out of a pig's bone, and cut through Augusta's burned skin. A long red line opened up on her palm like a canyon, and the woman moved Augusta's hand above the overflowing river, so that the crimson drops could drip into the water. At the same moment, the other guard loudly called out the sharkanj's name.

The wound was scorching. It wasn't enough that the cut hurt, but her skin was still unprotected, out in the open. A scream wanted to slip past her lips, but she managed to bury it deep inside. She used all her concentration to keep her face still, knowing that the women would report on her behavior to Mother and others, including Lana. There was no way she would let them speak anything but the words of highest praise for her courage. She promised that to herself.

Something flew out of the river, so fast all three of

them jerked backwards. The large, elongated body of a snake circled the air above them, agile and elegant, adorned with small wings, twisting so much it was hard to see where the head began and the tail ended. Water was dripping from the flexible body, landing on Augusta's uncovered face, burning her. The guards squeezed closer, while the snake continued constricting the circle of its body, as if it were a noose around their necks.

A broad head appeared right in front of Augusta. The shape of it fell somewhere between a snake and a wels catfish, flattened with whiskers—two long, twisting under the gaze, and four small ones, on the lower jaw, just like some women had short black hair under their chin—but there were fangs in the mouth, and narrow, snakelike eyes above it.

The head hissed, opening the gills on its neck like a fan. The sharkanj came so close to Augusta's face that his flicking tongue licked her cheek. She raised her eyes, full of defiance, looking the snake straight in its brown eyes. This close, she saw that the scales were the same green color of the river.

The sharkanj moved his head, spread out his thin wings, and relaxed his tense body, moving away from them. Only when he completely disentangled himself did he change, the snake body disappearing. In its place, a naked man stood, a little bit taller then Augusta, but still a bit shorter than her Mother.

He could've been younger than her, but also older. She wasn't sure how river snakes aged. Like dragons? Like humans? Like wels catfish?

"What clownery is this?" a soft baritone yanked her out of her thoughts. "Haven't I told your leader to leave me alone?" His voice had a gentle, syrupy note, but in a way poison might appear sweet—it was completely obvious that there was an underlying danger hiding there.

"We bring you gifts," one of the women said, finally jolting from her stupor. She wasn't going to cower under his hostile welcome, even though Augusta could see her hands were shaking slightly. The other nudged Augusta closer to the man. He looked her over, profoundly confused.

"I don't understand," he said. Up close like this, Augusta could see that he wasn't just lean, but also muscled, even though he was as thin as a blade of a seaweed she one saw on the gifs. His black hair was cut short and soaked through with river water, and it would've appeared the rain wasn't bothering him. If one took into account the fact that he stood naked while it rained, that is, without a blink of discomfort.

"I am the gift. And in the bag we have some food sent to you by our high priestess."

He opened his mouth, then closed it, then opened again.

Then repeated it again, until he finally spoke:

"And what, pray tell, should I do with you?"

He gazed at Augusta's escort, waiting for answers, explanations.

"Whatever you wish, sir. We're calling upon the old traditions. We're offering a sacrifice, for prosperity and the safety of our land—" one of them started.

"For the rain to be stopped," the other finished.

The sharkanj looked at one, then the other, his eyes spread wide. Then he opened his mouth and started laughing out loud. It didn't sound joyful. More like rocks so sharp they could cut into the skin on the soles.

"Sacr... I can't, do I look like a dragon to you? Go bother Azhdaya at Trsat!"

This was an answer they obviously hadn't expected. The two of them briefly glanced at each other, disoriented, and then one of them found her courage and said:

"We came to you, calling upon the sacred old ways—blood and a maiden sacrifice." With every new word spoken, she sounded more sure of herself. "We don't care what you'll do to her. Eat her, enslave her, it doesn't concern us. But you can't refuse the old way."

Standing so close to the man, Augusta saw the moment he pursed his lips in anger. For a second, she thought she could see lightning flashing in his eyes. Maybe it was coincidence—or not—but the rain started pouring stronger, ruthlessly banging on their protective clothes.

"*Old way*, you say. *I can't refuse*, you claim. And how did you choose this sacrifice, may you explain?" His voice dropped an octave lower, full of fangs.

"We held the lottery," Augusta jumped in, before the women could get a word in. She wasn't sure why she'd said that, skipping the part where she volunteered, maybe to see how he would react. Would that enrage him even more, or would it be pleasing? "Like in the old ways," she added, just in case he didn't understand her.

Thunder struck somewhere close by, and her guards flinched in surprise. Augusta, on the other hand, managed to keep her cool. The man smiled, showing off a string of white teeth.

"The lottery. But you see, that's not really a proper sacrificial gift," he was telling the women behind her back, holding them in place with his gaze. "Sacrifice has to come from the person that prays for something, not from someone else. So, if you pray for the safety, prosperity and the sun, I expect you're ready to sacrifice your own skin, too. Tell me, are you?"

One of the women threw a dirty look in Augusta's direction, meaning she'd relay everything to her Mother, but Augusta didn't care right now. She enjoyed their discomfort, the fear leaking from their pores. There was something immensely satisfying in the way the tables had turned on them. Augusta had reconciled with her destiny. But it was a mighty nice sight to see someone else getting cooked in the stew her Mother had prepared.

The other woman nodded her head. "For safety," she quietly said, straightening her back. This was, after all, one of the village guards. And she was simply doing what Augusta's Mother had ordered. If anyone was supposed to feel terror, it was Mother, not these two. The satisfaction Augusta had felt earlier dwindled and, in its place, a guilty conscience started to rise.

"So, let's see that," he said, with a voice that didn't leave room for discussion. "Take off the masks and the goggles, the gloves and the hazmats."

The women watched him in shock, but still obeyed without complaint. Slowly, they removed the raincoats from their bodies, and goggles and masks soon joined a neat heap on the ground; atop of it all, their lamps. They stood there in their clothes, with their heads uncovered in the rain that was falling over their foreheads, their eyelids, cheeks, lips and necks. One of them hid her hands in her pockets, the other one under her armpits.

"Now, into the river, the two of you," another command followed. Even though the rain had started pouring harder, while the light of the lamps was turned in another direction, Augusta could see how one of them started crying silently. The other bravely pursed her lips and went towards the river, swelled with the rain.

With every passing moment, Augusta waited for them to turn around and start running away. With each new step taken, she expected for one of them to break and start begging for mercy. But they were Mother's warriors and, like that, they went into the water without uttering a single word.

The sound of meat sizzling was surely just in her imagination. The sobs, on the other hand, were definitely real.

Tasting bitterness, she caught the sharkanj's forearm, clenching it. He was all bones, muscle and skin. "Enough. They didn't choose any of it. This was all my Mother's idea, the high priestess'. They are just following orders."

"And so, following orders meant bringing someone to the slaughter," he replied. He was watching her with an intensity that could've almost shamed even her Mother. Almost, but not completely. He lacked the unrestrainable power Augusta had learned to associate with her Mother and, possibly, the bora. "But, you say your own mother sent you? She either greatly cares to get my help, or has none of the care to spare for you. What is the truth, I wonder?"

Augusta swallowed her saliva, unwilling to answer that question. Not even wanting to think about that. The sharkanj probably noticed that, because he shook his head sadly, and moved away from her, finally giving her some personal space.

"You can come out now," he yelled to the women

in the river. "Get out of my sight. Don't you ever dare come near my territory again!"

He didn't need to say it twice. They rushed out of the water, covered in angry red blisters visible even in the near dark, and put the protective gear back on in haste. One immediately ran to the forest, half-dressed, dragging the rest of the gear with her hand, while the other turned around, looking at Augusta questioningly.

"You too, go," the sharkanj told Augusta, impatiently.

"I'm the sacrifice," she stated simply, gesturing with her hand for the last woman to leave. "I'm not going anywhere."

She didn't dare tear her gaze off him, but she still sensed the moment they were left alone. He started circling around her, hostile like before, just in his human form, this time. What should she do now?

"Is there something wrong with you? Do you wish for death so much? I gave you a chance to—"

"A chance," she interrupted him, with a bitter laugh. "I don't think you understand. They expect results. A lack of them would be unacceptable. I can't go back with nothing to show for it, *I can't.*"

Especially not when her escort will return with the tale of how she'd screwed them up with her loose tongue. She didn't even want to imagine how her Mother would react. The thought alone was nauseating, even more than the pungent smell of rain.

"I don't think you get the part where I don't want anything to do with you. I don't want to get into any sort of deal with your village."

"I'm sure you could think of a way I could be *useful*," she added hastily, getting into his face. The rain was now pouring steadily, and it was hard to shout over the river, so he must've misunderstood her because he replied, laughing:

"Not interested in women, thank you. It's not my fault your village follows some very narrow-minded traditions." His mocking tone grated her way more than the implication that her value might only be associated with sex.

"My village is desperate. Trust me, you're not the first one we've asked for help; you're not even our third option. But everything else was a bust. Our magic is too weak to stop something on such a great scale, and we have no one whose power lies in weather control. And this rain—it should've already stopped falling. The fact that it just goes on and on without end, that's not natural. Doesn't that bother you?"

As soon as he grinned, she knew she'd misspoken.

"Of course it's unnatural. Not a lot of things are natural these days. Everything went to hell decades ago, when the gods decided to play with our lives. So, tell me, why should I meddle in someone else's business, especially if there's a powerful creature behind this lovely weather? I could step on their foot, and for what? People I don't even like?"

"Because I'm absolutely sure you need something, too. Everyone lacks something. There has to be something I could help you with. Look at it this way. This is a deal you're brokering with me. Ignore my village. I'm the only one here. This rain—it's bringing harm to me, too, and I want it gone for my own reasons. So, please, do it as a favor for *me*, and, in turn, I'm going to do a favor for *you*. Whatever it is. I'm ready to do anything," she said, with a healthy dose of despair. It seemed he was lost deep in thought, but she didn't want to get her hopes up.

"Given who your mother is, you probably do have some magical knowledge, don't you? How strong are you?"

It was time for her to laugh. It was harsh, unmerciful—louder than the river's rumbling and the rainfall, probably scaring the forest animals to death. She was laughing in his face, and it filled her with great joy.

"I bring disease," she told him as soon as her burst of laughter stopped. Upon her proclamation, a dreadful silence burrowed into the ground and the tree roots, into the water source itself, rising up to the clouds and the sky, too. "I am the Disease," she added, just in case, leaving no room for misunderstanding.

The sharkanj blinked, a little surprised, but unafraid. He put the fingers of his right hand on his lips, his look calculating.

"And you're telling me that only now? They've sent me a gift equivalent to biological warfare dressed up as a maiden sacrifice. You know what? You're right," he said, a smile stretching wide. "I think there is something I could ask of you. There is, after all, something you could help me with."

Lian—as he'd introduced himself—decided they should continue their conversation as civilized folk, and invited her to his house. In his human form, he brought her to a stocky single storey house, situated dangerously close to the river bank, with solar panels on the roof and an old Tesla parked out front.

It was hard to miss that there was barely any rainfall over his house, only a few drops here and there, seeming lost. Also, although the river had swelled up on all sides like rising dough, there was a sense of restraint in the torrent, as if someone had twisted it in a tight knot. The effect was dizzying. The ground around the house was almost dry, and the building itself appeared pathetic, as if the design which had been used to build it was meant for a dumpster.

The inside was a bit better, mostly because it was obvious that it was lived in. The living room was narrow, adjacent to the small kitchen, and had an adorable quality to Augusta's eyes. The sharkanj, Lian, had left her there, while he'd gone to get dressed. So she used a moment to snoop. The couch was cozy, covered in colorful pillows. The gray walls were filled with shelves, some carrying books, some various other stuff, mostly cameras of all ages and types. Even though there was no organization to the clutter, it didn't look messy or like it cultivated new bacteria.

The kitchen had only two elements in it, one with a sink, a stove and a big fridge with a freezer. The fridge was a story in itself—littered with magnets which fixed polaroids to its doors. For a curious Augusta, it was a small, if not hidden, treasure.

Most of the photos were of landscapes—pretty boring, if you asked her—then some wild cats, looking like they were posing for a shot, and only two showed people. In one of them, she found Lian hugging some unfamiliar man from behind. Both of them were smiling, carefree in the shirtless shot. Lian didn't appear younger than now, but there were no hints in the house that there was another person living here.

The other photo was of some couple. The man had a strong appearance, looking like someone had shaped him from a mountain top. If she had to guess, she would say he came from Lika, but she knew it was only her wild association game combined with her own, preconceived ideas about what a person from the Lika region looks like. The woman, in comparison, was tiny but, given that the only other person in the photo was huge, it didn't mean she was truly short. Augusta assumed she was one of the Chinese people living in Rijeka, given her appearance. Because of the similarities between her and Lian, they must have surely been a family—maybe a son, a grandson or, hell, even a brother. She had no idea how old the polaroids were.

"Having fun, poking your nose into other people's business?"

"Yes," she replied brightly, twirling over to the now decently dressed sharkanj. "How old are these photos?" She indicated the ones she wanted to know.

He didn't look impressed. "Very old."

"Very old, as in, old like the first time the polaroids were in use, or old as in, when they got popular again before they got out of fashion for the second time? Although, given how preserved they look, I would say—"

"Please, sit down and stop talking." He sighed as if was suffering a great torment, and pointed at the couch with pillows. Shrugging, Augusta sat on the offered seat, getting cozy between a blue and a purple pillow. They were so soft that she was enjoying this immensely already.

"Do you live alone, or is your husband somewhere close?" She took a shot in the dark, hoping to uncover at least something. "Just so I know, in case I need to prepare myself. This whole maiden sacrifice thing is not something that happens everyday."

"You don't need to worry about that," he replied. "Look, just because we're going to do a favor for each other, it doesn't mean we need to be friends. All these questions are useless."

Augusta got more comfortable, if somewhat dissatisfied. She couldn't say exactly why she felt like that, but she still wanted something more than a simple business transaction out of this. Then it hit her, like lightning. This was the first time she was outside of her village, alone, in the company of someone who wasn't a part of her community. Who didn't know anything about her, or her family, or—

"What is it now? You look like you've just figured out you've left your head behind."

"Nothing. Just thinking." She frowned, slightly. "And this was a very specific comparison. Not really well done."

"Oh." He paused in front of his kitchen, his gaze switching between Augusta and his fridge, as if he wasn't sure what he should do next. "Do you want something? Tea, coffee? Water? I have the best filtered water in the region, trust me, I'm sure you haven't had anything this good yet."

"I thought I wasn't here for a friendly chat, but for the business deal?"

"This is simple decency, gods. Where did you grow up to mix up basic etiquette with friendship?"

"Maybe I'm just bad at jokes," she tried to feign at nonchalance, knowing there was some truth to his words. "And maybe I have no idea how friendships, or business deals, work. Choose for yourself what better suits your perception of me."

Lian rolled his eyes and sat down in the chair, straight in front of her.

"Then, let's get down to business. Before I tell you what I need, how strong are you? Can you cause epidemics or just individual sickness, non-communicable types?"

Augusta couldn't hide her surprise. She was certain there was nothing vague about her words in the woods. But, clearly, some explanation was needed.

"I'm the Disease, like…" She paused, searching for a name that wasn't the derogatory expression she despised. Rather, she decided to tell her story to illustrate; unlike him, she had no need to hide. "When I was born, almost half of the village got some sort of mutated pox. There was no vaccine for it. Highly deadly. A lot of people died, and probably more would've if my oldest sister didn't have the power to heal." Unfortunately, her sister had also been a child at that point, and there had been limits to what she was able to handle at that tender age. "I almost decimated my village, and I was barely out of the womb." She shrugged. "What do you think my range might be these days?"

She wasn't certain what she'd been expecting, what sort of reaction from Lian. But it was certainly not him nodding along, with a look of respect. As if he was going to… a nauseating thought passed through her brain. *Don't you dare say…*

"You're the Auntie Plag—"

"Do not call me that!" she interrupted him before he'd finished his sentence, disappointed. She'd expected more from him. Probably because he had no love to spare for her Mother, which she understood completely. "I hate that name. Besides, it's not ever correct."

"Okay, okay." He raised his palms up towards her, in peace. "I'm sorry. I'm guessing you didn't have an easy childhood after that."

At least his apology sounded sincere enough. She laughed without joy, aware she was probably looking like a sneering animal.

"To put it mildly. My sister told me that Mother had wanted to beat me to death with her own hands, but Aunt managed to get in the way." She desperately wanted to share her side of the story, outside of the village lore which got taken for granted. "Regarding the others..." She shrugged, aware that it had happened a long time ago. "The world was still recuperating from the Great Rift or whatever you call it. Rebuilding. Our village was doing the best it was able to with the new rules, finding ways to survive. And then I came along, making it worse. I'm not the most popular girl. Most people have either lost someone dear to them because of me, or they remember the dead, and the new generations learned to keep away from me." She lowered her eyes. It was getting harder to watch the sharkanj, unsure what would be worse, for him to pity her or to agree that she deserved it. "What is done is done."

She heard him hum, thoughtfully. Augusta observed the red spots on the pale skin of her right hand, the one that had been left in the rain. It was scorched and swollen, but the pain was already a thing of the past. The knife wound irritated her more, slashing her palm in two sides, like broken asphalt of the old highway.

"I was born as a snake." Surprise jolted her into raising her head. His look was full of understanding. "I admit my story isn't as traumatic as yours, except well, it had been, for my parents. It's not really easy when, instead of a human child, there's a snake slithering between your legs. And they say giving birth is hard on its own," he joked. She couldn't help, she laughed with him. When it passed, he went serious again. "To make things worse, before that, dad hadn't even introduced mom to his family... history? Situation? Genetics? Admittedly, he probably didn't believe baba, his own mother, himself, when she'd tried to explain what she was."

"Didn't believe her?"

"That was a bit before the gods came to us and started their magical infighting, left and right, in front of everyone. What did you call it? The Great Rift? I must confess, I haven't heard that one. Fairypocalypse is what they call it down in Rijeka."

Augusta did a quick math in her head. So he was older than her, at least a decade, or even more, depending on what a *bit* of time was for him. He just seemed younger.

"In any case, both of them had the shock of their life," he continued. "Dad fainted, allegedly. Who knows what mom thought, in that terrifying moment. Maybe there was a moment when they wanted to kill me, too. Although, later, they learned to deal. I can't say I lacked anything in my life, even when the world collapsed around us. Baba's power and status helped us a lot. But, regardless of how much they love me, I always have a feeling that, subconsciously, every time they see me they remember that first moment of pure horror when I was born. When they only saw a monster, not a child. That has to be deeply ingrained in everything they do, how they behave towards me, even if they aren't aware of it."

It was his turn to shrug. His eyes were dry, but Augusta was sure she wasn't imagining the sadness in his tone.

"Where are they now?" she asked. The way he spoke made it seem like they were still among the living, but she couldn't visualize the three of them living squeezed in his small house in the middle of nowhere.

She wasn't expecting him to answer, given his previous behavior but, after a short sigh, he obviously decided to satisfy at least some of her curiosity.

"While baba was dying, I had to come here, so I could take her place on the river. This is my true home. But I didn't want my parents to follow. It's too dangerous to live outside of the towns. This forest is full of wolves and bogeymen."

She nodded to show she understood, maybe even more than it had been his intention to show her. He had acted like he'd wanted to get rid of her as fast as he could, but he still brought her to his house, sat her down, and listened to her tale. Loneliness, her solitary, oldest friend, was something she recognized with no trouble at all, no matter how hard he tried to mask it.

She wondered what had happened to the man in the photo. Had Lian left him, too, for safety? In a curious turn of events, she decided to stop intruding. They both had a job to do. Her village depended on the sharkanj's task.

"I think it's time for me to hear what you expect me to do. You know what I want, to stop the rain. I can only assume what you might wish for. So, let me hear it. Whom do I need to make sick, and how bad does it need to be?"

Lian straightened in his chair and, in a serious voice, he delivered his request.

At the end of his speech, there was silence, not as uncomfortable or heavy as silences can go, even when it had every right to be. She should've taken the offered coffee when she had the chance, so at least she would've had something to do to fill the silence with. Instead, she scratched her burned hand, keeping her focus on Lian. He was sitting completely still, calmly waiting for her reaction. He didn't seem worried, at all.

"Why? If I may know," she finally spoke up.

Lian pursed his lips.

"Do you know anything about beluga sturgeons?"

Her eyebrows hiked high up her forehead. She wondered how stupid she'd sound if she admitted she had no idea what he was talking about.

"Er, no."

"Those gigantic, ugly fish? They live in some rivers? Living fossils? They used to be extinct in our region for a while. Still nothing?"

She shook her head. The fish weren't her area of expertise, too impractical for her village to even try to farm. They were too far away from the sea, and the closest river to their village had a guardian.

"Long story short, belugas are fish that live for a lot of years and they have existed since... basically forever. They were valued for their caviar, which is why they were hunted out. Ergo, that's why there were no beluga in our waters for some time. Sometimes, one would get back, but... that's unimportant. Now, some similar fish showed up in my river, except that their skin had, how should I put it, evolved. It changed, I guess, thanks to all of the magical waste. Or some creature made them that way, for whatever reason. You never know, these days." He shrugged.

Augusta blinked in confusion. Then twice more. Now she, herself, felt like a true fish out of water, twitching on the dry ground. "Evolved?"

"Turns out, their skin became... hardened, and resistant to the chemicals in the rain."

"Oh." Slowly, she started seeing what direction he was going in. It wasn't the first time she'd heard about an animal adapting to the magical world, and better than humans. And she had a pretty good hunch what that meant for some people. They were always trying to find new ways to protect themselves from the rain, faster to put on, easier to use, so they didn't need to depend on the factories to make raincoats for them. "Let me guess. They started to hunt these new fish for their skin?"

"Exactly. The poachers' camp showed up out of nowhere, recently. Cockroaches who came from the north. And they've started, without any respect for me or my territory, without my permission, to shamelessly hunt out these neo-belugas right under my nose, even after I've explicitly forbidden them."

"Why didn't you do something?" Her Mother wouldn't have tolerated this amount of disrespect, and would've already acted on it.

"You think I didn't want to? They obviously knew about me beforehand, because they came prepared. They have protections against my kind and..." He shrugged, angry and, it appeared to her, ashamed at his helplessness. "Alone, I can't do a thing. It's not like I have a lot of allies to help me." With that admission, he wiggled in discomfort.

"That's what you get when you don't want to cooperate with people. I know you don't like my village, but I heard your baba used to help us in our time of need. My Aunt always says that the biggest power people have is the fact that we are social creatures. That the only reason we've survive the Rift was because we were a group and—"

"That's all well and good, but I didn't ask you to evaluate my life," he interrupted her, disgruntled.

She shut down her mouth, deciding to keep the rest for herself.

"Okay, sorry," Augusta continued. "Back to the topic at hand. These poachers hunt in your river without your permission, and you can't do a thing against them. Still, don't you think that what you're asking of me is a bit... extreme?" That was the thing which intrigued her most. In the short amount of time she'd known him, she'd observed how angry he was over her village offering a human sacrifice to him, so she thought he placed more value on life. She thought him more merciful. She was, obviously, wrong.

"You don't know these people." His eyes flashed, and this time she knew it wasn't an optical illusion. She didn't need to assume where the thunder, which she could hear right now in the background, came from. "If you need me to ease your conscience—let's just say they don't deserve your tears. Their camp is one of those that make living outside of the towns dangerous. Do you need more than that?"

She raised her hand to put a stop to his angry rant. This was, obviously, a painful topic for him. "I just asked because I got the impression you're not fond of the suffering of innocents. You were pretty much abhorred at my Mother's behavior. But maybe I'm wrong. Maybe you just stayed on your high horse because you don't like us."

Lian opened his mouth, probably to snap back at

her, but something in her words must've struck a chord with him. He closed his mouth and shut his eyes, tiredly rubbing his eyelids. For the first time since they'd met, he actually appeared to be older, even more than the age he probably was.

"I know how my river breathes, as well as all that lives inside of it. I can feel everything the poachers are doing, and how they're doing it. All the spilled blood, completely in vain, in a world where we need to take care of it like the precious thing it truly is. And I can't do a thing. I've observed them, I've warned them. They didn't listen. The magical protections are making them arrogant. I didn't invite you into my house to discuss morality, but to do a job. Now tell me, can you do what I ask of you?"

She watched him carefully—his voice calm and his eyes dark like a turbulent river, full of emotion. If this was something he wanted, who was she to judge him? Her village would've cleaned the camp up ages ago in his position, and in a much bloodier way. They would've handled it like they did the thieves; like the one that was currently rotting in their stable. She remembered what Lian had said earlier. *It's too dangerous to live outside of the towns.* They were a people on the outside of the rules, except for those they wrote themselves. Some people were crueler than the others, especially if her Mother were to be taken into account.

She stretched out her legs in front of herself, knowing what she was going to tell him next.

"Can you do what we ask of you? Give us our sun back?"

Lian nodded. She stood up, offering a hand to him.

"Okay, then. Point me in the direction of the camp, I can do the rest myself."

She was singing inside her head while she walked, watching her step. Going through the branches and the dense forest, like a thief in the night. She wanted her walk to ooze with elegance, but if she were to stumble in the mud, it certainly wouldn't be graceful, even if there were no one there to see her. The events which were unfolding right now were too significant for her to turn out to be some klutzy villager.

She breathed in the acidic smell of the warm rain drizzling on her raincoat, breathed out with the forest around her. Every branch she passed by bent slightly, as if it were bowing to her. Except for the susurration of the river and the drops of rain, no sounds could be heard. The whole place had quieted, as if it were trying to appear invisible to her eyes. All the hearts in her vicinity were beating in a rush, loud drums setting the rhythm for her steps. She felt every animal in its hidey-hole, every blade of grass on the ground, each leaf on the branches. Life pulsed where she went, dancing with her goosebumps, smelling sweetly to her, like a poison.

Fear. It was fear that she was breathing in, that was leaking in the air. Even the rain had calmed down.

She wasn't walking as Augusta anymore.

She knew she'd approached her goal even before the camp itself materialized before her eyes. Hidden in a forest clearing, close enough to the river, but far enough that the poachers didn't need to worry whether the torrent would overflow. A protective spell circled the camp in a hoop, compelling her to end her journey before the invisible line. It covered a big radius; she'd been stopped far enough out of the camp that they probably wouldn't be able to see her, not in these conditions. It would seem it wasn't placed just against the sharkanj, but against anyone who might come uninvited.

Frowning, but not giving up, she circled around the camp, following the invisible thread. Maybe it was already broken someplace, or she might find a weakness to exploit. When she came back, full circle, it already seemed that her taking on her primordial role would all be for nothing. That, she didn't like. The protection around the camp was of the most common kind, too general and vague to really hold. There had to be a way for her to step over it. The forest hummed in suspenseful anticipation.

She sat on a bare rock, mulling over possible strategies, when, suddenly, there was a movement inside the camp. Among the old caravans, with tarp-covered solar panels on their roofs, in full dark and in complete silence, a shadow was moving. Someone was walking with haste, hunched down. They couldn't hide from Augusta, though, in their conspicuous orange raincoat. Following them with her gaze, she stood up. There must have been a way for her to use this, and pressure of anticipation rose in her chest.

The shadow was moving further away from the camp, only to stop at the protective circle. Augusta hid close by, between the trees, waiting patiently. The man, if she needed to guess, was watching the forest before him, and then looked behind his shoulder, at the camp. As if he were uncertain. This could be her weakness. Unless the man simply turned around and went back.

She licked her lips, waiting. Time slowed down to the drops of rain on the leaves and the shuddering of a stranger.

Finally, after what seemed like a whole hour, the man raised his foot and took a step. Then another. He lit up a dim blue light on some device she couldn't see, and took another one.

And found himself outside of the circle which had protected him from Augusta.

Carefully, so as not to startle him, ready to strike at any moment, collecting her power under her fingertips like a subtle flow of a cobweb, Augusta stepped out in front of the stranger.

He was young, confused, and frightened, as far as she was able to see under the artificial light. His eyes widened as soon as he saw her, but not so much in fear, as in a genuine shock over her unexpected appearance.

"Where to, at this time of day? And in this weather?" she asked gently, trying to sound harmless. Just a young woman on a stroll in the woods. She smiled, kindly, innocently, without a care in the world.

"Wh... what are you doing here?" the young man asked. He gazed towards the camp, then back at her. His eyes told her a story of fear. "It isn't safe here." But not because of her. His eyes were big and beady, making her think of a bunny running away from wolves. When she approached him, she could see, under his blue light, a bruise under his eye, and a cut on his cheek.

"Who did this?" She raised her arm, wanting to touch his purple eye, but the man visibly flinched, as if he were expecting her to hit him. So she simply lowered her hand.

"Doesn't matter. But you can't be here... please... you can't... you must..." His words were growing mumbled, incoherent. He looked, again, back at the camp, like he was expecting devils themselves to get out of it and start running after him.

"You are afraid of them, but you're from the camp. Aren't you?"

The young man lowered his head in shame. His hair was hidden under the hood of his raincoat, but a solitary lock fell over his eyes.

"I'm not... I... my family is there. I... don't know where to go, actually. I've never dared to try to run away. Where would I go? To Rijeka? To Senj? Out to sea? I... I just don't know..." The sentences hung in the air, flowing like smoke from an open flame.

"What do you want to do?" To her, it mattered whether he would change his mind and get back inside the safety of the spell, or if he would choose to stay the course, and try to run away.

He shrugged, still hesitant. "I don't know." His eyes watered, ready to cry. He was watching her with a plea in his eyes, as if he were waiting on her to deliver him from his troubles.

"Why tonight?" she remembered to ask. In the air, she could feel the intensity of her purpose, the electricity of anticipation, the life of this young man in her hands.

"I don't know," he repeated again, and again, but, this time, he was staring in the distance behind her back, lost in thoughts. "I couldn't sleep. I've been unable to sleep for days now because I feel... here, somewhere—" he touched his chest "—that something bad is going to happen. I can't bear it anymore. Yes... yes, I need to find the strength and just run away. I'm a grownup, I can take responsibility for myself and my deeds." He found her eyes, this time with certainty.

"It looks like you've found your answer," she said, amused. He was either clairvoyant or there was some other sort of magic in place, protecting him. Even so, he obviously didn't know how to use his power, or didn't even know that he had it, since he didn't look like someone who could protect himself. And then, maybe it had been destiny to make the two of them meet now, right at this moment.

"Listen. There's a... safe house, nearby. You can lie down there and catch up with all the sleep you've been lacking. And tomorrow, or some other day, when you're feeling up to it, you can calmly think about where you want to go, what to do next. I'll help you get some food and things to barter with. Maybe I could even get you a lift to Rijeka. You don't need to be alone in this. But..." She stopped when she saw how he'd brightened up at her words, and let it sink in. "I need something from you in return."

"Of course, anything, just... I just want to get away..."

"I need your permission to go into the camp. You need to invite me in, so to speak."

He was surprised; she could clearly see it in his face. He blanched, as if it had dawned on him, for the first time in their conversation, that there was something strange in her showing up at this time. In her appearance. Lost in his own troubles, he didn't even notice how odd it had been that there happened to be a young girl strolling through a dark forest this night, in the toxic rain.

"But why... I said it wasn't safe in there. The things some of them are able to do..."

"Hey, hey, it's alright. I know what I'm doing." She tried to sound as gentle as she was able to. He was still more afraid of what they might do to her, than vice versa. She put her hand on his cut cheek, slow and kind, but with enough pressure to remind him of his wound. "Do I have your permission to get inside your camp? Can I enter your home?"

The man was completely lost. Under her touch, though, he nodded, almost imperceptibly.

"Yes. You can get inside. You are," he breathed in, loudly, "welcomed." Exhaled. The thin line blocking her way snapped, as if cut with scissors.

Augusta smiled encouragingly. She lowered her hand from his cheek and gave him detailed directions to Lian's house.

"And don't forget to tell him that I sent you there," she said in the end. "That you have my protection, and that you are a part of the deal I have with him. Do you understand?"

"I understand. Thank you, thank you," he took her by her hands, tears on his face, and repeated, "thank you."

She patted his hand, and then removed herself from his arms, pointing at the forest which she'd come from. But she made no more than two steps towards the camp when she remembered something.

Turning around to the man who was bracing himself for a trip through the dark forest, she called out to him. "Is there someone... you would want to be spared?"

Bewildered, he looked at her, then at the camp in question. But he didn't need to think too long. "The last camper, the one with the black door. The shoddiest one, obviously patched. It won't be hard to miss."

"Alright." She dismissed him with a smile.

Then she went into the camp, now open for her path. Feeling heaviness in her arms, she took off her gloves and her raincoat, freeing her long black hair from its braid. She could feel every drop of rain on her skin as if it were a fiery kiss of a candle, while her white, ceremonial dress from the lottery clung to her body, soaking wet. She even took off her boots, lowering her bare feet onto the waterlogged grass, scorching like live coals. From her hair, she took out the withered rosemary stem, crumbling it in her palm. No matter the warm rain, or the pungent air, heavy like a handmade, feather-filled quilt on her skin, she only felt ice in her blood and bones.

With a deep inhale and exhale, she started counting her steps, approaching the sleeping camp.

With the first step, she was able to imagine bile in the mouth, risen from the stomach. With the second one, bodies started convulsing in their beds. With the third one, everything stiffened, constricted. She entered the camp with the cacophony of drumbeats in her ears. With each new step she made, the melody was getting quieter. Everywhere around her, lungs were collapsing, and sleepers slept about drowning, seeking another breath, trying to catch it with their hands, only for it to stay out of their reach. Under her fingertips, she felt rotten skin as she breathed in the smell of decay. Suddenly, one of the doors at her right opened, and someone stumbled outside, visibly drunk.

He was watching her with wide eyes, broad shoulders, and clenched fists; with a huge hunting knife on his belt. He wasn't wearing an orange raincoat, but a snug jacket made out of some sort of leather, with a hood. She remembered Lian's fish.

They were standing like that, gazes locked, when the man staggered on unstable feet over to Augusta, grabbing the handle of his knife with a crooked smile.

She calmly stood her ground. Not moving a muscle, not even blinking. Her long wet hair lay motionless at her back, a black cascade on white clothes.

The knife was the first thing to fall to the ground, completely useless. The man followed then, landing on his knees, vomiting before her feet. The liquid flowed from him as steady as the rain, and when there was nothing left for him to get out of his stomach, he started throwing up blood and teeth as his body hit the ground, spasming until the last organ failed and the man, dead, went still in his own vomit.

She stepped over him and his bodily fluids, and continued on, undisturbed. Everywhere she went, people dropped dead; only the last house, with patches and a black door, was spared to see another day.

Her burns stung in the sun, even under the calming balm Lian had fixed for her. She should've really taken cover in the shade, instead of sunbathing on the grass. She itched everywhere, but there was something very welcome, and even sweet, in that sensation, knowing that she'd played a big part in getting this lovely, sunny weather.

"I suppose you're quite satisfied with my work?" she heard Lian's voice. When she opened her eyes she found him standing above her, still a little green in his face. He hadn't completely recovered from fulfilling his part of the deal. She'd been unable to see exactly what his snake form had done, flying in the clouds, but ever since he'd landed, he spent a lot of time lying down with nausea, which was why it seemed to her like he'd drank down all of the rain. Nevertheless, he looked better now, than the night before.

"Are you satisfied with my work?" she returned in kind.

"Yes; except, of course, the part—" he slightly nodded at something on his left "—where you've dropped an unwanted guest to me."

She followed his nod and saw the young man from the camp, who'd introduced himself as Ferdo, tinkering under the hood of Lian's old Tesla. At exactly the same moment, his head emerged. He caught their gazes and smiled under his russet locks, stopping to wave at them. Augusta and Lian raised their hands and waved back. Happy, Ferdo resumed his self-imposed work, while Lian turned towards Augusta, his eyes narrowing.

"What? He played a key role in my deed. Plus, you could always chase him away," she said, smiling innocently, knowing full well that he had no such plans. Lian sighed, rubbing his eyes. He'd relayed to her what happened when Ferdo had first come to his doors, shuddering with fear and lack of sleep, constantly repeating her message. How Lian had found, while helping him to take off his toxic clothes, more bruises and old scars.

Lian sat down on the ground, near Augusta, and stretched out his legs on the grass.

"And I see you've gotten quite comfortable here, too. Why haven't you gone back to your home yet? You did what you were supposed to do. You're under no obligation to stay with me. Shouldn't you end your story the same as every other hero who returns from his quest, marries the princess, and gets the kingdom? Or in your case, the village?"

Augusta closed her eyes, fantasizing over his words. Her heroic return to the village, as a savior instead of the monster who'd hurt them with her birth. She could hear their shouts of joy, see all of the people gathered out in the field, reaching towards the cloudless, sunny sky. There would be Lana, her whole face radiating happiness, hugging and kissing Augusta. She imagined her Mother, nodding at her in respect, making her a promise that, when she died, Augusta would inherit her seat on the council. It was such a pretty image. Exactly what was expected from a story, as Lian had noted. She wasn't ready for the sure disillusionment which was waiting for her upon her return, to see her hopes dissolving, like smoke.

"And leave you to handle the lost puppy I've found in the forest on your own? Come on, not a chance." She opened her eyes and smiled, showing off her teeth. "Anyways, I found a prince, or a male maiden—what would be a term for that?—from the stories, the one intended for marrying in the end, except he's not for me."

Lian rolled his eyes, but she knew she wasn't imagining the slight blush on his cheeks.

"You're talking nonsense."

"He could've gone on already, you know. I offered him that. Instead, he's over there messing with your late grandpa's car, and I'm pretty sure he doesn't know a thing about cars. Otherwise, he wouldn't be searching for the engine under the hood."

Ferdo really did do his best to appear working, but he spent most of the time just looking at the car, hands on his hips, a wrinkle on his forehead.

"He's only here until he recovers, and he doesn't want to be useless. I just think he wants to give something back for room and board. So leave the poor guy alone, you understand?" Lian's voice was strict, but lacked real emotion at the same time, like a dull blade. He would never admit it to Augusta but, even though he'd spent most of these last few days lying on the couch as if he were struggling with sea sickness, he appeared much more cheerful than when she first met him. Much more talkative, too. When the two of them leave, everything will return back to how it had been. Lian will be a lonely river snake, while she will continue to be her village's persona non grata. Who knows what will happen with Ferdo.

She frowned at the thought, disliking the direction her mind had gone, when the day had started so nicely.

"I'll leave him be, and in the meantime—" she rose up from the ground "—I think I'm going to deliver him from his pain and suggest we all take a walk by the river. I think it will be good for you to stretch your legs a little. I can see you're not as green around your gills anymore," she joked. He looked so affronted, reminding her of a plucked chicken, that she burst out laughing.

The day was too lovely to use it on dark thoughts of the future. Whatever happened, there would be time to think about it. For now, she decided to enjoy the fruit of her labor and soak in the rays of the sun, knowing that, back at her home, the preparations for Midsummer Eve were surely underway, everyone content and safe under Mother's watchful eye. Augusta's sisters were probably with the children, outside, finally allowed to play in the field, instead of a stuffy hall. Lana was, no doubt, relishing the sun, just like Augusta was, under the clear blue sky. And, she guessed, her Aunt was checking over the panels, sunbathing her shaved head. That particular thought hurt, so she buried it down.

There was already too much rain in her life. Now was the time for some sun, even if she needed to make it stay.

The Rock at the Bottom

IN THE BEGINNING, THE villagers brought cats—newborn kittens, collected in a bag—to a small island that could be seen from the mainland. Not big enough to use for pasture or for cultivation, so it was left to the reign of thorny underbrush overgrowing sharp, salty rocks. People would gather in a procession, in their Sunday best, a bag of thrashing and mewling furry bodies in the hands of an elder. They would sit in their boats and row to the island in the middle of the night, torches fixed to the bows, illuminating the dark.

They would never stay for too long on the island, before they crept back to the boats, going back to their village a few felines shorter, but richer in the crops for a dozen years. With time, the cats stopped doing the trick, so when the land started giving sour, sickly food, dogs followed, and after them, even sheep. Whatever it took for the land to be plentiful; tomatoes ripe and red, the zucchini bigger than the forearm, grapes juicy and sweet, perfect for winemaking. Enough for the liters and liters of rich olive oil, flowing like a river, which got sold to the bigger villages, towns and inhabited islands, because they had too much. When war or famine hit every other place in the vicinity, only this village stayed untouched by any horrors of harsh life. And for such a small price.

A bag of newborn kittens. A strong dog. A sheep or two lambs.

Until that stopped being enough, too.

The scorching sun fried Luka's skin, even under layers of tan. His vision swam, head full of cotton, mouth completely dry. A playful conversation could be heard from the upper floor, his wife's sing-song voice a melody that turned sour in his stomach. His mother was up there with her, talking about... something. He'd heard the beginning of the talk by staying directly under the huge windows, which were covered with a light mosquito net. But if someone were to ask him to repeat what he'd heard under duress, he wouldn't be able to unstick his thoughts enough to remember.

He stood like that, in the vegetable garden, his hands shaking, unable to move away. They will surely see something was wrong, or ask him what he was doing. And he would not know where to even start with answering that.

Two more years. It was supposed to wait for two more years. Luka had begged Kate, when she'd first come up with the idea for them to marry, to wait until the twelve years' cycle had passed. It wasn't that long of a wait—they were young, barely out of their teens, it would be easy to wait for two more years without people raising eyebrows.

Kate hadn't agreed. Her parents—much more strict than Luka's—were already putting pressure on her to find a match. Not only that, but people would take notice if they got married soon after the Giving, and get it into their heads to punish them for cheating. Or, worse, if there weren't enough pregnancies—a year before the Giving—they would gather all young unmarried couples and force them into marriages whichever way they saw fit. So, Kate had reasoned, it would be better for them to marry right away, some two and a half years before the Giving, and have a child as soon as possible. It would put their families in the clear. No one would suspect them of trying to skirt the village rules. No one would suspect they weren't so devout. And most importantly, she'd said, no one would look twice at the two of them, and wonder if there was something different about them. Something *wrong*. Something that would paint them as useless to their community. *That* would land them on the boats, faster than anything else.

If they couldn't contribute in one way, then they would contribute in the other.

There was an anxious lump in his chest during the first few months of their married life, from wondering whether they would be able to get pregnant on Kate's timetable. That sort of thing didn't always happen just by saying it. Some couples tried for years. The two of them were blessed, they'd believed, when it happened without a hitch, and now, his heavily pregnant wife was laughing with his mother in their bedroom.

Luka, on the other hand, stood in the garden, neither fish nor fowl. Slowly sizzling on the burning sun.

In his hands, he held a zucchini, cut in half, the insides only a rotten, black ash.

"Are you sure you want to do this?" Ema asked, not wanting to be a party pooper, but also not really keen on her girlfriend's plans. Laura obviously didn't hear the note of concern, because her grin was wide, untroubled.

"Come on, where is your sense of adventure?!"

Ema didn't want to say, *buried under financial dread,* mostly because this trip had been *her* idea and she didn't want Laura to feel guilty. And it really didn't have anything to do with Laura's newest plan, because that one was actually low budget. So she fixed Laura a reassuring smile, hoping it would be enough to fool her girlfriend, soon-to-be partner for life in the eyes of Croatian law. Or *wife*, like some people would call it, if it weren't for some foolish laws about the *definition* of the word 'marriage', passed a few years back.

"It's just that it's been a very long time since we've spent the night on a beach. I'm not a teen anymore." Even though calling it a 'beach' was somewhat generous. The small island was visible from their spot at the derelict port, completely empty of boats, which was somewhat curious given that they were in Dalmatia and, nowadays, every available scrap of sea shore was turned into profit. They could swim to the island on a floatie, so close it was. Still, unless it hid some gorgeous sandy beach on the other side—fat chance—they would have to lie on the hard rocks. But Laura was giddy with excitement, bursting with joy the whole week of their trip, so she'd come up with this questionable wish. To spend the last day of their vacation on a completely barren island. Just the two of them, the sea licking at their feet, the stars twinkling in the wide open sky above.

Like they did that night when they met like college girls, partying at some music festival by the beach.

Ema understood sentimentality. It was the whole point of this trip. A few months ago, when she got the rare substantial payment for one high-profile project she did, it wasn't even a question over what she should do with it. The smart thing would've been to save the money, of course, for there was no way she would get that much again for her storytelling or from book sales. But there was a time to be smart, and there was a time to be happy. And making Laura happy was, in turn, making her happy, too.

This was the last day of their vacation, she shouldn't mope because of sharp rocks. Or worry too much.

Even so, no matter how much she smiled, or thought positive thoughts, every time she glanced at the island's one old lonely lamp, she couldn't shake the feeling she was looking at only one part of the story; a dangling, illuminated antenna of a ginormous anglerfish, hidden in the depths of the sea.

The damp basement reeked of vine, olive liqueur and moisture but, to Luka, it mostly smelled of death. He knew it was in his head, because he'd inspected the whole place up and down, including the smallest crevices, looking for dead, rotting mice, hidden behind old cabinets, oars, barrels—almost completely drained—a variety of gardening tools and a huge fishing net. He found nothing except cobwebs and dust, while his father sat at the small table, watching his jittery movements.

Still, the smell clung to his nose, a rotting, sour scent of a dissolving corpse.

It got only worse when others came in and opened the wines and liqueur, alcohol permeating the air, tingling his nostrils. His stomach clenched, half-ready to just get everything out of it—some salty fish he ate for lunch, before Kate had gone wide-eyed, gasping. Which promptly brought the meal to the untimely end, when it finally dawned on everyone that she'd gone into labor. Everything after that had been a flurry of motions, and Luka got delegated to the basement with his own father who kept clapping him on the shoulder the whole time. Now Kate's father joined them with some of his own friends—two old, but rock- strong fishermen—and even Andrej came at the rear, who played the role of Luka's best man. If he weren't there, smiling from ear to ear, toasting to Luka and Kate, it would be taken into account and, sooner or later, people would ask questions, searching for gossip. If they couldn't find any, they would create some.

It was easier to act like everything was alright, even though every jape Andrej said felt like a punch in a gut. Especially because his laughter was wild and boisterous, but his blue eyes stayed cold as ice.

"Here, a drink for the soon-to-be father." Roko—Luka's father-in-law—pushed a glass overflowing with crimson wine into his hands. Roko's two fisherman friends flanked Luka, each on one side, with toothless grins. Making him feel trapped, even though he was in his own basement, at his own table. A fish being circled by sharks. Luka tried to smile, hiding his discomfort, swallowing only a small amount, unwilling to end up passing-out drunk.

"Not yet," Luka added after a sip of wine. It was bitter, with a hint of sweetness, and it fell on his nervous stomach as hard as a rock. Nausea hit him hard, a lump in his throat so big it felt like he would choke on his own vomit before he managed to get anything out.

"But soon enough," Roko continued, pouring an olive liqueur shot to himself. But he didn't down it, like he usually did. No, Roko tasted it, but the miniature glass was still mostly full, and his murky brown eyes never left Luka's. He was a huge, meaty man with a bulging stomach, his one arm as big as Luka's two, his bald head glistening with sweat under the lamplight. Luka became acutely aware that, if this man wanted to break him, he would have no problems doing that. Especially not with his two friends, who could easily hold Luka between them. Surely they wouldn't dare to do anything in front of Luka's own father and Andrej, whom they all knew to be close to Luka?

Except that Luka's father, who sat quietly, drinking down glass after glass, was already half drunk. Luka's father was always uncomfortable near Roko, as if he'd done something wrong by letting his son marry into Roko's influential Arneri family. They've held the prestigious elder circle spots ever since the dawn of their village, most of the time being at the head of the procession for the Giving. Even though Roko wasn't yet an elder, nor were the Arneri the leading family for the upcoming celebration—that would be the Nobilos—Luka's father never could quite relax.

Andrej on the other hand, was a whole, electric ball of nervous energy, something Luka could recognize by sight in the way Andrej's leg twitched under the table. He would jump to Luka's defense, not caring for his position in the village, but at what cost?

Luka was losing his mind. He imagined he could hear Kate's screams, which he could not, and smell some phantom corpse; his insides were tangled in a fearful knot.

The zucchini in their fields had already turned rotten, one by one, and people were scared that the grapes and the olives would soon follow. Just yesterday, a dead fish had surfaced in the sea, scaring some children. The villagers were whispering and everyone was waiting for an official proclamation from the Nobilo family or other elders. But there was still none; no one said anything about holding the Giving earlier, even though more and more people muttered that, the sooner they did it, the better for everyone. Luka could see the glances of his own neighbors, anticipation barely hidden on their faces. There was only one other baby born recently, and in the Nobilo family, with just two other pregnancies, not counting Kate's.

"Your face looks green," Roko noticed, smirking under the dim yellow light. If there were a secret elder meeting underway, would Roko know? Roko's great uncle held the seat; surely he would slip in front of his great-nephew, who'll soon become a grandfather, whether there was a real danger for his family or not. Even though Kate is not an Arneri anymore, she still counted. Didn't she?

Would Roko leave them hanging? *He would*, a voice whispered in Luka's head. If this were happening at the eve of the true Giving, Roko would not bat an eye if his grandchild was chosen at random for the ritual. Like he didn't when his own first wife was accused of trying to run away pregnant. Luka had been a child when it happened, but he would never forget the smell of the bloated corpse, locked in a cage on the port. The baby survived in the end—Kate's oldest half-brother, one of the strongest men in the village—while some other baby was put on the boat instead.

"You should really drink! Let the women do their work and, when you wake up, everything will be done, and your life will be richer," Roko's boisterous voice shook the basement to the foundations. Or at least it felt like that to Luka, who felt like a branch caught in a storm, sitting there. Roko's friends laughed with the big man, the one on the right clasping his shoulder, the one on the left nudging a glass at him.

"A lot can happen," that left one said. His voice scratchy from smoke, he sounded like someone's nails trying to break open a coffin's lid—from the inside. His foul breath, smelling of tart onion and tobacco, hit Luka in the face. "It's better if you're not all here when that baby is out."

There was so much wrong with that sentence, but Luka swallowed his disagreement. It didn't feel smart to try to argue that he wants to be there for his wife because something could go wrong. They would just point out he wouldn't be able to do anything, or that his place was not there, or something like that. That he needed to leave birthing to the midwife, who was, truly, more than capable. For everything else, there were Luka's mother and mother-in-law up there with Kate, helping. But it still felt wrong.

Luka turned towards his best man Andrej, trying to find a friend under that sharpened blade of a smile. Someone who would be on his side. But Andrej shrugged, raising his own glass at Luka, before drinking it all out. Their recent quarrel fresh between them, an open wound full of salt.

"It can last for the whole night," Andrej finally told him, his voice rugged, but still a balm on Luka's tortured thoughts. "You can sit there and worry the whole night. Or you can try to relax."

Roko nodded, slapping his palm at the table, shaking it. "Listen to your friend. He knows what's what."

For just one moment, Andrej's eyes lost their wall, letting Luka glimpse at the bleeding hurt inside, before it froze over once more. Just an iceberg, nothing more. "Once the baby is born, you'll never stop worrying. It will be your whole life." Andrej's voice was like a bucket of freezing water, pouring all over Luka's head. Chilling him to his bones.

The panic turned into a throbbing headache, his thoughts constantly running in a circle. No one said anything about the Giving, he just had to remember that. He was just jumping to conclusions, making himself ill with his thoughts. It wasn't right. He clutched the damp glass, forcing it to bring the bright red wine to his mouth. His hand didn't move. The glass stayed on the table, mocking him.

"So, Andrej, we heard you're thinking about going away?" Roko's question hit Luka as hard as lightning. Fast and unsuspecting, burning him.

Leaving him a dead husk at the table, a puppet on strings.

Luka brought wine to his mouth and took a big swig. He didn't stop drinking until he lost track of everything. The talking, the glasses, the faces of his drunk-blind father and Roko and the fisherman; until he put his head on the table and gave up consciousness, too, the smell of death rocking him to sleep.

"I'm sad she will not know what we did. That I got to see her hometown, swim in the same sea she did as a child." Laura's voice sounded far away, melancholic, like it usually got when she talked about her grandmother. The old woman had been a pivotal person in her life, the first of Laura's family to accept her unconditionally when she came out.

Ema remembered her as a short, stocky woman, wearing all black, her eyes the deep blue of an underwater grotto. She hasn't been the sort to back out of a fight, ready to throw hands even, an epitome of *meet me at noon, pistols at the ready.* When Laura's parents refused to acknowledge Ema as her girlfriend, it was grandma Luce who'd welcomed her with arms wide open, inviting Ema to family meals, excitedly talking about folklore and old stories, always praising Ema's work. While simultaneously doing a whole passive-aggressive routine with Laura's parents, saying that it was better to annoy them than try to beat some sense into them with a spatula.

She hadn't deserved to wilt away from pancreatic cancer. Ema squeezed Laura's palm in her own, to show Laura that she understood.

They were lying on the beach, or what passed for a rocky beach on the uninhabited island, their bellies full of grapes, cheese and sweet white wine, content. As Ema had suspected, there wasn't a hidden paradise here. The word *island* was even, maybe, stretching it too far; she would rather call it a glorified rock. The only reason they didn't walk all its length was the thorny shrubbery growing wild in spots. But there was a clearing where the old kerosene street lamp awaited, alone—probably a form of a lighthouse, where some poor sucker had to row over here to just light it—and they'd docked there in the rented kayak.

The beach was littered with washed-out debris from the sea—plastic trash, probably from boating tourists, and broken branches—where Laura and she chose to camp out for the night. A small gravel path passing through the undergrowth, leading to the probable center of the island, made for the most interesting part. It looked like someone had dug out the rocks in a circle formation, making a hollow spot in the ground. Not big, but wide enough to fit a bag, or maybe a small animal. There were strange white stones put on a pile like a low wall around the hole, guarding it from the undergrowth. Looming over it, a completely white tree stood there, bare branches pointing to the skies.

"What do you think this was supposed to mean?" Laura asked, completely in awe, her curiosity so real Ema could taste it as strongly as the salt in the air.

"Who knows, maybe that was some sort of attempt at making a well?" It was a weak explanation, and Ema knew it. The shallow hole and the dead tree were unnerving her, making her palm itch with the need to cover the hole up. She could almost hear a soft mewling sound turning to cries, and she shuddered at the sudden cold breeze blowing from the sea.

"I just wish grandma got the opportunity to come here again," Laura mused in the present.

"Do you think she would've wanted to see what has happened to her village?" Ema carefully asked, something she'd been wondering most of their vacation, but felt unwilling to broach the topic before. Now, when the sky was turning the color of a runny egg above a mountain on the horizon, while the sea brushed over the rocks in a lulling lullaby, while the last day of their vacation was turning to night, she thought she could ask it without fear of souring their trip or grandma Luce's memory.

"Hm. I don't think she would. Not really." Laura sighed, and sat upright, turned over towards the mainland. The mountain dominated the view, one of the high tops dedicated to an old god, then stolen in the name of a saint when Christianity conquered these lands. Ema could see a small chapel, perched on the steep peak. At the sea level, lights started twinkling into existence; signs of life from a village where they'd booked their accommodations for the duration of the trip. Once upon a time, it used to be a miniature village suffering from famine, but with time, this whole region had become popular to the point that the village had grown into a tourist trap. Full of ugly, high apartments, gray blocks of concrete that grew like a tumor and overpriced restaurants on every step. The port was riddled with boats and cruise ships so you couldn't see the sea in front of you. While Ema and Laura slept in their Airbnb apartment, they could always hear movement—local drunks singing into the night, teenagers and children screaming in play, a variety of languages of the passersby, even in late August, after the official high season had already been declared closed.

It was a complete opposite image of the one that had waited for them in the place where grandma Luce had spent her youth. They had to book an apartment one village over because grandma's village didn't really exist anymore. It was a ghost town, great houses left to desolation. Their solemn beauty had marred with time—white rock turned dirty gray, gardens overgrown and wild. The fields above the village had completely reverted to the hard, unforgiving ground where only sickly tomatoes grew, reeking of pus. Olive trees were dead and white, completely dried out. They'd passed through the narrow stony streets, looking for the house where grandma Luce had been born and raised for the first few years of her life, knowing they might be able to recognize it by the octopus mosaic on the façade, tentacles following the doorframe. It should've been easy. But all of the houses were similar—huge, two storeys, closed off with fences, decorated with mosaics which had started falling out under the stress of the winds and the storms; yards full of debris. A few of them had octopuses, obviously a popular motif, as were the fish, olives and grapes. Grandma Luce had been too young when her mother took her and relocated to the north of Croatia, as far away as they could've gone, meaning her memory of the place had been too vague, so her stories weren't the best to orient themselves with once they were on location.

"I think this would've made her even sadder." Laura's voice was full of longing, not for the lost place, but for the lost soul. The golden hour illuminated her face in the soft glow, making her look like a renaissance saint. "I mean, it's not like she'd been in contact with her remaining family, with her mother very effectively breaking all contact when they moved away. Grandma wasn't stupid. She told me she knew something rotten had happened between her mom and the others, and that the village probably wasn't the happy paradise of her childhood memories. I think grandma never tried to visit here precisely because there was part of her that knew she would be disappointed. So she rather kept the idealized version, instead of seeking the truth."

"Maybe it was better like that," Ema concluded. The truth was ugly, abandoned houses and barren fields like someone had taken a torch to them before pouring salt so nothing would ever grow from the land again. It was such a stark difference to the flourishing tourist village the two of them stayed in, that you had to wonder how not one of the descendants had tried to use their property to try to revive it, since everyone with extra cash poured into the whole region in the summer. It surely wouldn't be that hard to renovate an old house and turn it into a rentable place. But, for whatever reason, no one bothered.

It was puzzling and, because it made no sense, Ema had kept feeling like she was walking over open graves while they'd been researching the place. When they'd asked about it among the old people of the neighboring village, they couldn't get clear answers. For hundreds of years, grandma Luce's village was the richest place on this part of the coast until one day, they weren't. There was something wrong with the land—it became impossible to grow healthy food and some sickness passed through, devastating the vineyards and olive groves. People started dying or moving away, until there was no one left. One sunburnt old woman had said that even the fish they'd started bringing out in the nets back then were all wrong, mutilated, half eaten, or poisonous, but Laura obviously didn't believe that one. Ema wasn't ready to disregard that tale, with the village looking like a corpse of a stone-made ancient god. She absolutely had no problems imagining nets full of acidic aquatic life, fish with mangled fins, or hatched without eyes.

That was the only reason she'd cut out a small branch of a holly oak they'd found on one of their walks, on what Ema dubbed the 'healthy part' of the coast. The mountain peak once dedicated to Perun—the old Croatian god of storms, thunder, sky and oaks—was still towering over them, and she hoped he would turn a blessing eye towards them while she held onto the branch.

"I don't know how to thank you." Laura turned towards her.

"You know you don't have to," Ema said, and meant it. "I'm glad we got to do this. It was truly one of the most adventurous vacations we've ever gone on." It wasn't a lie, even if, most of the time, she felt like at any moment they would stumble upon a dead person boiling in the sun.

"Even if it was way too expensive?" Laura worried at her bottom lip, and Ema touched her cheek to comfort her.

"So what?" Ema asked. "It's not like we can afford to visit some fancy place like the Maldives. We can at least visit the beauties of our South, even though people here can get..."

"Bigoted? Yeah."

"The point is," Ema leaned in, with her face close to her girlfriend's, whispering like someone could overhear them on this godforsaken rock, "I want our life to be full of adventures. Since we can afford it, why not? Besides, I wanted to give you an early wedding gift."

Laura's face beamed at Ema, her blue-green eyes glistening in the sunset. "I love that word."

"Wedding?"

"No, gift."

Ema snorted, but Laura leaned in all the way, silencing Ema with a kiss. In that moment everything faded away. The worries, the abandoned places, the fear of freezing her butt off in the chilly night out, the weird not-well and the dead tree guarding it. There was only Laura, her blond hair catching the setting sun, turning into living gold.

Life turned into a sort of haze for Luka, a perpetual hangover, even though he drank very little after that time in the basement. The baby was born healthy, no one tried to steal her away and people came and went, congratulating them. Kate was dead tired and he was completely useless the first morning of his daughter's life but, nevertheless, he tried to help out as much as he could.

Months passed and nothing happened. Instead, the grape harvest gave the best fruit, promising to become the good wine. People were delighted. Joyful. He couldn't match their mood, dragging around, feeling like a huge rock was dragging him to the bottom of the sea. Slowly drowning him.

There was a big celebration for the christening of their baby girl, but Kate had a fixed, sad face the whole day, her eyes always turned towards the island which was their blessing and a curse.

"You don't need to worry," Luka tried to tell her while he gently swayed their baby in his arms. "No one talks about doing the Giving ahead of schedule anymore."

"Of course not." Even though Kate's words were agreeing, her tone was biting, like a freezing winter storm. "Why would they? Whatever sickness plagued our zucchini is gone," she said, but it sounded like a curse on her lips. Not even the cooing baby in his arms could soothe his troubled thoughts after that.

"What's wrong, then?" he asked, with a heavy tongue.

Kate's face fell, her body slouched, overcome with tiredness. "Why do you think something's wrong?" she countered, but it didn't feel overly convincing. Before he could answer, his mother came into the room, rushing them to get ready for Church. What a sad farce that was.

Kate and her melancholic moods weren't the only thing bothering Luka. Andrej was avoiding him like a plague-carrying rat, while preparing to set out the sea. North Africa, he'd heard by the power of village gossip, the rock on his chest getting heavier. Every day he woke up, he was an inch deeper underwater, breathing harder. Until one day, he would sink to the bottom, unable to take another breath.

"I'm sorry," Kate told him one day, while nursing their daughter. At that point, Luka was so lost in his thoughts he almost didn't hear Kate lying in the master bed, looking at the wall, but not seeing it.

"About what?" he asked, his mind already counting the fish. He wondered if it would be better if he took a big stone the next time he set out fishing, and tied it to his legs before throwing it overboard. But he couldn't do that to his baby girl, or to Kate. There would never be a fairy tale love between them, but they had been friends ever since childhood. He had a responsibility towards her, no matter the truth of their marriage. Besides, without him in the picture, the village would just force her to remarry, against her true wishes. He couldn't do that to her.

"I'm sorry for chaining you to myself," she finally answered, her green eyes watering. "This was such a selfish idea."

"What are you talking about? I agreed."

"But if you hadn't, you would be free now, getting away from here with Andrej." That last part hit him like a sudden waterspout in summer.

He shook his head, wanting to get away from that bad feeling which had been following him ever since he'd opened that rotten zucchini; wanting to get rid of it.

"Don't say that. This was a good idea. Hey, hey..." He got out of the bed and knelt close to her, where she was sitting in the rocking chair. Luka put his hand on his daughter's head, caressing her little tuft of hair. "Who knows what would happen if we hadn't married. But I know one thing for sure. We wouldn't have her."

At that, Kate burst into tears, shaking so hard it upset the baby. Soon, the daughter joined in her mother's crying, while Luka crouched there, feeling so out of place, he could've easily been in another body. Unsure what to do, he hugged Kate, gently rocking her, like she was a child herself.

After that, everything took a turn for the worse. Kate walked around like a ghost, with only a half-focus to life, her face constantly shadowed with regret. Luka's mother said it happened sometimes to new mothers and that he didn't need to worry too much. His father, on the other hand, just ignored Kate and him altogether, even though they lived in the same house. At some point, a huge storm brewed over, forcing them to stay put in the house, the sea boiling over the beach and the port in waves so big it looked like it would drown them. The shutters kept knocking all night, getting almost ripped away at the hinges. Luka spent the night comforting his daughter, who was inconsolable, her wailing trying to compete with the mayhem outside. She was afraid, and, in turn, he felt helpless, knowing there was no way for him to explain that everything was alright, that she was safe. That her father was with her, taking care of her.

Too concerned about his daughter, Luka couldn't fall asleep, so he heard when the front door opened. He rushed out, fearing the storm had finally managed to knock the power out, only to see Kate outside, in the yard, screaming towards the dark sea, the waves rising so high it looked like another sky.

"Take me, take me, please!" he heard her beg in the rain, lashed by the wind and the water from both the clouds and the bay. Luka took her in arms, her body drenched. Kate didn't try to fight him, but she didn't stop crying either, her tears mixing with sea salt on her face.

The commotion woke up others in the house and his mother worriedly ran out to help them, only for Kate to refuse her."No, not you," she thrashed in Luka's arms, while they were getting inside the house. Trying to get away from her mother-in-law.

He didn't have time to get confused, he just asked his mother to leave them alone. He helped Kate out of the wet clothes, her skin so cold it felt frozen. No amount of blankets helped to get her warmer, her lips getting dark blue, almost the color of plums in a tree. He tried to move them towards the kitchen where he could get a fire going in the hearth, but she begged him to stay in their room, with their baby girl.

By morning, she was already worse for wear, unable to get out of bed, in fever. One day turned into two, then into a week. The whole time, Luka was stretched thin, taking care of his daughter and his wife, in a constant state of panic. Feeding his daughter with goat's milk, since every time Kate came to, she begged him not to let their daughter out of the room, or to put her in a stranger's hands, or let anyone hold her who wasn't him. Fear was overcoming him, covering him from head to toe, turning him into a nervous wreck who was constantly looking behind his shoulder. Waiting for a hidden blade to stab him in the liver. He couldn't give into it, though, so he closed it deep into his heart, not really wanting to think too far in the future.

His parents tried to help but, after Kate's outburst, he didn't want to let them near her. It didn't matter why she was scared, or what was happening inside her mind; he'd seen genuine dread and hurt the night of the storm, and he wasn't thrilled with making her feel like that ever again. Kate's mother came to visit, too, or at least tried, but Kate didn't want to see her either, no matter how bad she was feeling. Kate's father, Roko, came by only to scold Luka; how he was a failure of a husband and a man, how he shouldn't let a sick woman order him around. If something were to happen to Kate because he didn't let other women help, he'd said, it would be on Luka's hands. How, if that were to happen, there would be no force that could stop Roko from breaking Luka's neck.

Luka stood his ground. In response to Roko's lectures and threats, he just closed the door in his face. To his mother's imploring, he simply stated that Kate's wellbeing was more important than what any one of them thought should be done. And if Kate didn't want to see anyone except her husband, daughter and the village doctor, so be it. They just had to deal with it.

After two weeks, Kate got better, the fever withdrawing, her breathing turning healthier, losing the rough gasps which had sounded like her lungs were pierced. She could sit and eat on her own, starting with a warm fish soup he cooked for her. Her green eyes got their focus back, and she was able to hold their daughter in her hands again.

"Will you tell me what's bothering you?" he asked, once it seemed she was much better. She was sitting at the window and brushing out tangles from her long, blond hair. At his question, she put the brush down in her lap, her huge eyes full of sorrow.

"Do you ever feel like, no matter what we do, we just can't win?" She nodded in the direction of the island, sitting innocently out in the bay, with its new lamp burning to illuminate the way for the Giving, and a hidden, shallow sacrificial pit calling for more and more with the passing of time. Soon, they'll need to widen it, so a whole, full-grown person could fit in there. "Sometimes I feel like I'm living on the web. I know there's a spider somewhere out there, so I try not to move, thinking maybe it won't know I'm there. But it still creeps closer, so sometimes I move around, to see if I can break free, but it only alerts the spider to my position. No matter what I do, whether I stay still or try to get away, it closes in on me, slowly but steadily. Until it comes upon my immobilized body and finally delivers me from this agony."

He could see it as clearly as if she'd conjured the spider in question just with her words. His own skin was crawling with the phantom tickling of a hairy, pointy leg prickling him in the back. Luka flinched under the weight of something intangible, but real.

"For me, it's the sea," he said. "I feel like something is dragging me to the bottom, a chain, a rock, an anchor. My descent is terrifyingly slow, so I can feel every moment of my drowning. I can't break free; I only know that, sooner or later, I will hit that bottom, and only that would be the end of it."

Kate nodded, sadness dripping from her gaze like bitter olive oil. "I told you, you should've run away with Andrej."

Luka shook his head. "And leave you here? No way. If I'm getting away, you are, too."

She laughed at that, her voice trembling in disbelief. "With what money? It's not like we can ask our parents, they would never let us out. They might let you go, but not me." *Not someone who could birth possible sacrifices*, was left unsaid.

"We'll think of something. Why not? I... I will find us a way... to get away," he promised, feeling lighter as soon as he said it, chuckling at his own bad wordplay. Just the idea that they could move, run, that they didn't need to spend their life in constant fear, gave him strength. He would do anything in his power to make sure that his daughter would never feel what her parents felt, to be put in a situation where someone got to choose between the life of her baby or other ones. To be constantly watched, judged, forced into a procession of blood. Or worse, chained to someone she couldn't love or tolerate.

Deciding to do something and actually doing it were two different things. However, just having a goal different from waiting for death to catch up to him, changed the way Luka held himself in the next few weeks, his thoughts clearing from the bleakness. Even Kate found new strength, getting out of the house, drinking in the spring sun.

He was in these high spirits when, one day, Andrej came to his house. As soon as Luka saw him, after enduring the months of avoidance, he felt shaken again. Unsure on his own legs, like a baby goat. It didn't help that the other man was obviously agitated, his eyes shifting over, unable to stay focused on Luka's face.

Luka brought him to the basement, where he was certain no one would overhear them. It hit him that it was the last place they'd spent some time together, the night his daughter was born. When his father-in-law had kept pouring him new shots, toasting to the father-to-be. While Andrej was constantly grinning like a shark, full of anger and hurt.

"Did you notice that you're losing parts of your octopus?" was the first thing to come out of Andrej's mouth, so awkward it made Luka sigh. Andrej was never like this, usually so confident, or at least acting the part, while Luka was the one who floundered.

"Yes, it wasn't good work to begin with, so we lost some pieces in the storm. I'm planning on fixing it, but maybe I'll tear it all down and simply redo it." He crossed his arms. "Andrej, I know you didn't come to discuss my wall. You've been avoiding me for months."

The fight they'd had before the night Luka's daughter was born felt, at the same time, as something definite and yet completely unfinished. The avoiding didn't help; without a chance to move on, to heal the wounds, it just let them fester. "I heard you're thinking of moving," Luka said when it became obvious that Andrej was still searching for words. Shifting his balance from one leg to the other, standing by the same table they'd drunk at their last time together.

"I didn't come here to talk about that. But the offer still stands." Luka had to fight an urge to frown, not wanting to get into another fight. It was the reason why they'd started fighting in the first place. Andrej had begged him to jump ship, but Luka hadn't been ready to run away at that point, nor did he want to leave Kate at the mercy of their community.

"You know I can't. I have a child now."

"We can take them, too," Andrej suddenly said, turning towards him, a fervor fueling his moves. "The four of us, we can run away together!"

Luka laughed, a bruised, hysterical laughter, the sound hurting his ears. It pained Andrej too, his face falling.

"Like they would let us. We wouldn't get far before they caught up with us." And it wouldn't end up well for either Andrej or Luka. They would separate Kate from them, a precious possession of the village while she was of childbearing age, capable of having a child over the next two Givings. The two of them, though, they wouldn't be kept safe. Luka knew what happened to those who didn't adhere to the village rules. The cage rusting in the water, the slow, drowning death, the corpse left for months until the small fish ate all of it.

"We could go first, send money back to Kate, secretly, find someone who could help her get away when she saves enough. Let people gossip that you're planning on building your own riches to buy a seat among the elders."

That plan didn't sound that bad, and it could be what Luka was looking for. He put a hand on his lips, his eyes searching Andrej's agitated face. "You weren't happy, originally, with the idea of Kate running away with us."

Andrej lowered his head, unwilling to meet Luka's gaze again. "I was jealous."

"But..." Luka stopped, feeling so surprised for a moment he couldn't find his voice. "But you know... you knew why we've done what we have. You said yourself it was a good idea, that you would do it, too."

"I know," Andrej agreed, his face turned downwards, "but it still hurt. And I know I said it was a good idea because, at the time, I thought it was. But the night of the marriage, when I was relegated to the sidelines while we all cheered the happy couple, I couldn't help but think, 'why couldn't it be the two of us?'"

It was hard to watch Andrej, red-faced in shame, otherwise taller than Luka, now hunched so much that he looked shorter. Luka let out a sad exhale. "You know why."

"Aren't you tired?" Andrej asked quietly. "I know I am. Constantly. I don't want to feel this way all the time. I refuse to believe this is the only way we can live. That's why I'm going. And I hope you'll come with me. We won't leave the girls behind, I promise, and I'm sorry for being such a jerk before. I was jealous but, honestly, now I'm just so tired. She doesn't deserve this shit, either."

Luka nodded, his head swimming with the new information, torn between feeling hopeful and fearful. Whether he should be relieved or concerned, even more. This didn't magically heal the rift between Andrej and him, but everything was easier with Andrej on his side again.

"That wasn't why I came here, though." Something in Andrej's voice cut through Luka's growing hope. He was twitching again, souring any relief Luka might've felt a minute before, turning it into apprehension. Something wasn't right.

"Spit it out."

"I..." Andrej stopped, his eyes pleading. "I need you to know I didn't know. I just need you to know that, before I say what I have to say. I promise you, I didn't know. I was angry, and hurt, but I would never be that evil."

A pit that had already been in Luka's stomach for months turned into a whirlpool. He remembered Kate's spider, while Andrej looked at him with a crestfallen face, so unnatural for his usual boisterous self. The spider was so close that Luka could feel its mandibles on his neck.

"What are you talking about?" Luka asked, but a part of him knew. A part of him had known the whole time.

"I was with—" Andrej closed his eyes for a moment, regret obvious on his face "—Ante, Ante Nobilo, and the only reason I'm telling you this is so you know it comes from a credible source…"

Luka couldn't breathe anymore. He was sinking deeper, the seabed so close he could see the sand. *The midwife's son.* The only reason Andrej would be bringing that up…

No. "Please—" *don't* "—tell me. What did you learn?"

Andrej took a deep breath before putting his hand on Luka's shoulder. Kate's sadness, her unwillingness to let their daughter out of her hands, to let either of their mothers near her, it was all coming down on him, the tiny little pieces making a mosaic. He had been so oblivious before, because he was focusing on parts, instead of the whole picture.

"They were ready, had a whole plan in place, and no one knew, not Kate, not you, they were even ready to get rid of you if you turned out to be a problem…"

"*Please.*" The drop to the bottom wasn't as painful as he expected. It didn't feel like anything, just water rushing into his lungs, overcoming all sensory input except Andrej's voice.

"You had another daughter. Luce wasn't an only child. In fact, she was born second, a few minutes after they stole her twin. Your firstborn. To do the Giving, in secret."

Ema woke up abruptly, from a nightmare she couldn't really remember. The cold breeze licked at her uncovered face, while her sleeping bag had managed to keep her mostly warm. The rocky beach underneath made for a hard bed, her body now sore as if she'd turned into a wooden plank just by lying on it. But it wasn't discomfort nor the chilly air that brought her to consciousness. It were the needles in her arms and legs, that feeling of complete paralysis brought only by pure dread. She blinked the last of the sleepy oblivion from her eyes, for the first time noticing a strange orange light, illuminating the spot where Laura and she slept. It was the old kerosene street lamp, raised on the island, the flame in the glass polyhedron the only source of light, since the sky was completely dark gray, without stars or the moon to shine above them.

"Hey, Laura," Ema quietly said, her gaze glued to the impossibly lit-up lamp. It was the sort someone had to light up for it to work, with a flame on a huge stick that could reach the wick in the glass box. "Hey, Laura, are you awake?" Silence answered her.

Her gaze finally peeling away from the lamp, she turned to Laura to wake her up. Only to be met with an empty red sleeping bag.

Ema jumped, her whole body on alert. *She'd just probably had to pee*, Ema told her own, beating heart and screaming mind, *don't overreact*. But if that were true, Laura would've just gone to the nearest bush, and when Ema looked around, she couldn't see her girlfriend anywhere. She was alone, under the inviting light, beaming through the opaque darkness that slowly fell on the island. Half of the mainland visible from her spot was also drenched in black, the other half littered with small, yellow lights which were slowly twinkling out, one by one.

Ema stood up, only now noticing the sea—calm on

the surface, so dark it almost looked like the sky had fallen into the ground. And yet, under the orange glow of the lamp, she could glimpse at the shadows beneath. The tumultuous forms forming, growing, twitching, swimming, coming near the surface, then disappearing in the depths again. Ema took a step back, putting some distance between herself and the water, acutely aware that she was surrounded on all sides. That there was no way for Laura and her to cross to the mainland except the kayak, which could easily be overthrown by a hit from below.

Digging out the twig from holly oak from the bag, she put it in her pocket, glad she was wearing pajama pants, expecting for it to get colder outside on a night in late August. Just touching the wood calmed her a little already, but the fact that she couldn't really see the mountain peak under the condensed darkness—like the sky itself was seeping a squid's ink, overwhelming the stars and the moon—was vomit-inducing. She had to swallow discomfort and bile, knowing she had to keep a clear head. When all of her mind just wanted to scream loud enough for the people on the mainland to hear her.

Thankfully, there weren't a lot of places Laura could've disappeared to. The moving shadows in the sea stole Ema's attention again. Unless she'd gone under the surface, of course. That thought alone could force her into a panicked mess, so Ema turned her back to the water and the shapes hiding there. She wasn't going to jump to conclusions, not until she checked the whole island, small as it was.

She left the quiet whispers of water licking the rocky beach behind and followed the path leading through the underbrush, now nothing but a black, unidentifiable mass. As her legs moved, so did the light, expanding with her steps, as if she was carrying a torch in her hand. Her jaw hurt from tension, her skin tingling with goosebumps. Her short-sleeved t-shirt was't enough for this chilly night air, but it wasn't the weather which had her feeling so cold. She should've never agreed to this, feeling in her gut that something was so very wrong with this place. If something had happened to Laura because Ema had been willing to tune out her own discomfort, close her eyes before obvious warnings, she would never forgive herself.

Not long after that, feeling like she'd had to walk for miles anyway, she came to the clearing, with its small stone formation and a dead, white tree. She stopped in her tracks, uncertain what to focus on first. The tree begged for her attention the most—huge, sinewy, blooming with small green leaves and full of dark olives, so crammed on the branches it looked like the tree was riddled with tiny tumors. It grew over the clearing, having no business looming that much for an olive tree. But she was more interested in what was under it, than the tree that should've been dead suddenly turning alive.

In the middle of the man-made hole sat Laura, hunched and squeezed in, a little too big to fit. She was turned away from Ema, looking towards the tree. Her long blond hair had a strange amber hue under the orange light. She wasn't moving, or making any sound, just sitting there with a calm so profound it felt adoring, devout. Ema swallowed the fear trying to slip out of her mouth. Her body wanted nothing more than to run to Laura and drag her out of that pit, but her brain closed down on it, cautioning vigilance.

Ema creeped closer to Laura, circling the pit so she could get in front of her. Laura was basking in the light, a golden beacon in the night. Coming in front of her meant getting under the olive tree, and Ema had to be careful not to touch the round, fruity pimples, or the branches. She had to crouch, thankful for a calm night, without wind. She kept one eye on the tree like it would reach with its limbs towards her, and the other at Laura's immobile body.

At some point she decided to crawl, and like that, on her arms and knees, she finally made it to the other side of the pit.

Laura's eyes were opened, but glazed over with a white film. Her expression also had a dreamy quality, unaware of anything. Her kneeling girlfriend in front of her, who was slowly trying to get her attention. The strange events. It was as if she were still sleeping, even though her position had to be uncomfortable. So twisted to fit, she looked like a figurine forced back in the yellow plastic egg inside a children's chocolate treat.

"Laura..." Ema whispered, but it was so quiet she herself almost didn't hear herself. Afraid to make any louder sounds, any sudden moves. Her body had frozen over, paralysed in fear, aware of the blackness closing in on their little orange bubble. Aware of the sounds that were slowly getting in her range, penetrating the quiet stillness of the island.

The mewling of cats, turning into screams that sounded like children being slaughtered. Steps on the rocky path she'd walked herself not a minute before. A gurgling murmur, like someone was drowning. A rising tide of noise, coming into the clearing, from the same path she'd come down by. Her back was blocked by a tree. Where would she even go? There was only more sea behind her, as it was around her. Besides, Laura was there, sitting in the pit, without any sense or knowledge of what was happening. Ema wasn't going to leave her alone.

On her knees, she crawled backwards, deeper under the branches, sharp rocks sticking to her palms. From the darkness of the path a small green body emerged, walking on all fours. A slender, elegant cat, its fur completely wet with salt water, the eyes glowing in the dark. It screeched like a broken record, drawing nearer to Laura and jumping on the rocks circling the pit.

More felines joined, their fur a similar green, the color of olive oil, slick from the sea. Their tails dropped water droplets with the motions, left and right. They jumped on the rocks, they hissed and screamed, some even fought, but mostly they circled Laura like prey. A fish caught out of water. Ema put a hand over her mouth, trying to be completely still, even though she knew they could see her in the dark with their beaming little eyes. They didn't care for her, though. Some of them even came close to where she was kneeling under the tree, their sharp claws extended out of their paws, ready to slash. Only to turn away from Ema, disinterested.

After them, something bigger came, and she almost didn't recognize the shape in the dark. It was huge, sturdy, like a lumpy stone that was somehow walking, completely green, as if it were covered in moss. Except there was a snout protruding from this stone body and majestic, spiral horns adorning it. It was the horns, which were perfect for ramming, that finally helped her recognize she was looking at a ram whose wool was so overgrown it covered its head and legs. It stopped near

Laura, who didn't even blink at the commotion. Some cats even jumped on its back.

Following the ram, new shapes emerged, and the sight made Ema gasp, regardless of her fear. They were people, if she could call them that. They were tall, green-skinned, completely naked and covered in dripping water and hanging seaweed, tangled in their long green hair which almost touched the ground. They walked in a procession, the first two holding a shining rock between them, illuminating the clearing in a sharp whiteness. It was hard to say how old they were, their skin smooth, faces angular and sharp as a shark's, eyes reflecting the lights like those of the felines. Behind the pair with the rock, others opened and closed their mouths as they walked, letting out strange, gurgling sounds, like a song in a language she couldn't understand. She could see pointy teeth in their jaws, perfect for tearing out flesh. The teeth of predators.

The pair in front must've seen her, but they didn't react. They just put the glowing rock on the pile of other rocks, before joining the others, turning their muscular backs to Ema. The clearing was too small for all of them, but they still continued to gather. Their clicking song was overcoming every other sound, like waves in a storm. They filled the space with their tall, slender bodies, their eyes burning in the night like fallen stars. She could see the claw like nails at their feet and hands, images of dead, shredded sharks clear in her mind. Not one tried to interfere with Ema, even when their eyes swept over her.

One of them—by position, she thought it must've been one of those who had carried the rock—spread their arms, making a screeching sound. It silenced the others, even the cats. Everything stopped. It was so silent, Ema could hear her own heart's beating, and the rush of blood in her ears. She couldn't see Laura anymore. Couldn't see the way for them to get clear from this mess. She didn't have any weapon on herself. The only thing she could do was pray, to any god who could be listening.

The person who held the others' attention continued to move their arms, their shoulders, and their head. She could see only their back, the hair completely covering it like clothes, but the others watched with the intensity of people who understood every move, every twitch. Some even nodded, joining in with their own hand gestures. Were they signing? Ema thought, her fear put aside for a moment, fascination coming in. She thought that the sounds they made were a language but, the more she observed, the more it looked like they communicated with the movements. Like sign language. Unlike any she'd seen. It wasn't Croatian Sign Language, that was for sure.

For a moment, she hoped everything would be alright. That this was just some strange occurrence, a misunderstanding. Some sort of festival for water people, one which Laura and she had stumbled upon completely by accident. By the time they stopped signing, she managed to convince herself that everything would be okay. They had language. They obviously had symbolism, rituals. But so did humans, and there were a lot of them ready to do unspeakable things to each other.

At some point the group started trickling out, walking away one by one, followed by the cats. Until only the first two, the sheep and Laura were left in the clearing. One of them turned towards Ema, their eyes finally catching hers. They were so strange, reflecting with every move but she could still feel them seeing deep inside her. For some reason, the person—a woman, maybe, it was hard to tell—looked similar to Laura, even with different coloring, the sharp teeth and the claws. There was something in the shape of their eyes and mouth, curved sweetly, almost innocently, a look full of longing and wonder. They bowed to Ema, a slight acknowledgment of her presence, the seaweed swaying with movement.

The other ignored Ema completely, reaching out with their hand to Laura. Ema's breath caught in her lungs, blocked by a blooming dismay. While Ema watched, Laura finally moved, first just by turning her head slightly towards the outstretched arm, then by curving her lips into a blissful smile, her eyes still glossed over with thin white film. Then her arm, accepting the offered one. It was like some old movie, where a gentleman helps a lady to her feet. With fluid motions, Laura stood up and the water person holding her hand brought her to the sheep, waiting calmly. Helped her get onto it, like on a horse. Once securely up, the pair of green people helped guide the sheep around, one on each side, flanking Laura. They started after the retreating procession.

Ema crawled out from underneath the tree, only distantly aware of the soreness in her limbs. She passed by the glowing rock, feeling the burning light on her skin. As she followed the group, her fingers grasping the oak twig in her pocket, her mind bustling with questions. Not *who* or *why*, so much as *how* will she get Laura back? For whatever reason, they weren't interested in her, leaving her alone. A part of her doubted they would've looked at her so calmly if she were to try to take Laura from them. They'd put her almost devoutly on the ram, walking by her as an honor guard. The whole procession was slowly getting to the beach, walking into the sea with purpose. Her panic was starting to overcome her senses, clouding the mind.

One by one, as they came, so they went. Cats jumped up with elegance, their slender bodies reminding Ema of otters, before they dived in. The water people followed, throwing themselves into the sea. Their long hair floated on the surface for a few moments, like poisonous algae. Behind all of them, the last two creatures with the ram and Laura in tow, came to the shore.

Ema found her lost voice the moment one of the ram's legs grazed the sea. "Laura!" she screamed, disregarding her own safety. There were still a lot of people close to the surface, shadows shifting under the light of the orange lamp. However, she couldn't let them just take her love with them, drowning her. Laura showed no signs of hearing her, her head held high, her arms crossed over the horns of the ram. Her guards did hear, though, and they turned towards Ema, their emotionless faces reflecting the red glow in their eyes.

"Laura! Please, wake up!" she yelled, and rushed, hoping she could get to the animal and pull Laura off its back, no matter the danger. But one of the persons walking by came to stand in front of her, catching her in their arms. They opened their mouth, showing the rows of sharklike teeth.

"Let me go," Ema thrashed in their arms, the ram slowly disappearing in the water. The waves grew and licked at the overgrown wool, rising towards Laura's legs. "Laura!" Ema screamed, her voice carrying over the surface, probably all the way to the mainland, but not to Laura's mind. "Let me go, please, why are you doing this?!" Ema screamed at the person holding her. It was the one she'd thought looked like Laura, but now, there was no similarity, nor could she understand how she could've seen some before. Their face was so sharp and blank, not much different from the stone they'd left on the island, except for the beady eyes of a fish.

They held her in a strong embrace while shaking their head. The bushy, drenched hair moved with fluid motions under the heaviness of the water. This close, she could smell the stench of dead fish, salt, and blood.

"You can't have her. Why are you doing this?" she begged for understanding from a creature that probably couldn't understand. "You can't have her, do you hear me?!" Her screams echoed in her ears like she was in a chamber. The sea continued devouring Laura on the ram's back, bit by bit. From her legs to her waist, raising over her chest, arms, and shoulders. Only then did she turn her head towards Ema and, with a small, blissful smile, her head submerged.

"No! *No!*" Ema screamed, and her captor must've thought she could do no more damage because they let her go.

She ignored them, running at the dark sea, condensed with dancing shadows. She couldn't see what was happening below, couldn't see the seabed, but knew it was full of sea urchins. Unwilling to step into one blindly, she threw herself into the water. She dived into the complete darkness, her body jolting away in shock. She resurfaced with a cry on her lips, swimming further away from the shore, before taking a deep breath and diving in again.

There was no way to orient herself, no way to understand what was what and where, in this realm of muted colors, without light. She could only feel movement near her, above her, below her, shapes brushing over her. Small teeth nibbling at her skin, knife-like blades slashing through her clothes. Her lungs screamed for air, so she changed direction again, ready to resurface.

Something, someone, caught her in their arms, nails piercing the skin of her arms. Dragging her deeper towards the seabed. She screamed in pain, feeling bubbles on her face more than seeing them. Her chest was crushed under pressure, begging for air. There were more arms at her legs, touching, scratching, the metallic taste of blood even on her tongue, mingling with the salt. With her free hand, she grasped at the twig of the holly oak and poured all the belief in old gods she could muster into that one frail piece.

Piercing light flashed through the dark, illuminating the shapes of the water people around her. She jerked her hand, stabbing the closest captor in the eye with the twig. They screeched with the unholy, gurgling sound, getting away from her, letting her out of their arms. Ema tried to move; but there were still more creatures nonplussed with what she did. But the light struck again, and the one that had held her on the beach swam to them, showing a sign with their arms. Others let her go at that moment, and, finally free, she shot towards the surface, grasping with her arms, her head almost blacking out with the burning in her lungs. She broke free of the surface, gulping the air in hungrily, crying in despair.

The sky was riddled with lightning, and she'd resurfaced in the midst of where bright flashes were hitting the sea. The smell of ozone permeated the air and she screamed at the mountain, at the sky, at everything and everyone that could be able to hear her.

"Help me! Help me, please!" Blood poured from her wounds, a huge spot of deeper darkness expanding from her—even her mouth was full of it. She stretched her arms out, directed her eyes towards the mountain peak. "Take me, instead, leave her be!" Ema begged and closed her eyes. Her arms and legs tired, slashed, weeping blood into the dark sea.

A flash of light, a smell of burnt meat, a sensation of the whole body set aflame, roots of the fire spreading and engulfing every inch of her until the pain was all her mind could understand.

They talked. They planned.

Nobody had known about the early Giving, except for a handful of them. It had been done in secrecy, so people wouldn't freak out, so there would be no panic. In times of great turmoil over the sea asking for bigger or earlier sacrifices, there was a fear of mutiny, of the possibility for families to be overturned. That wasn't what either the Nobilo or the Arneri had wanted. So the village was getting ready to hold the Giving on the old timetable like nothing was amiss. Pregnant couples were getting anxious, putting on a brave face, all of them hoping it would be someone else's baby, not theirs.

Luka knew better.

So he talked.

So he planned.

The pressure of constantly holding himself under control was getting on Luka's nerves, but he endured. His head was much clearer than it had ever been. The chains drowning him were still there, but he was not alone. There were people that he loved who were keeping him afloat, but what gave him the most strength was rage. The need for revenge. To hurt back.

It wasn't an elegant solution. It wasn't even pretty. It was definitely missing the beauty of the ritual. He wasn't wearing his best clothes, nor were Kate or Andrej. They didn't gather in a procession or hold burning torches. But the food was great, the best Kate had ever made, the bread spongy and soft, perfect to collect the juices from the fish soup. The fish was tender and almost sweet. The cookies, on the other hand, were hard, tasting of walnuts and almonds. The wine was freely flowing into the glasses, as it had been the night his daughters were born, only for one to die before dawn.

It was a family affair. Kate and Luka had brought both her parents and his to the table, so they could apologize for their apparent abysmal lack of respect, shown when Kate was sick. They also had an announcement to make.

Kate stood up in front of them, her glass held high. "We will participate with the next Giving," she said in a clear voice, "God saw to it." And if they drew the wrong conclusion from the words, or the hand she held on her belly, who could blame the two of them? Kate said what she said, and Luka grinned the widest grin he could muster, showing off his teeth.

He smiled all night, while their parents slipped into unconsciousness, falling face-first into the plates. His grin was fixed in place even when he let Andrej into the house, to help him with the heavy, limp bodies. Luka's father might've been thin as a twig, but Roko was shaped like a boulder and weighed more than a barrel of wine. Their mothers were also both stocky, heavy enough for the two men to break a sweat. Under the cover of night, one by one, they dragged the bodies into Andrej's fishing boat. Kate stayed on the pier, a silent watcher of their trip toward the island.

They didn't bother with torches. They didn't even row all the way to the island. Instead, they stopped in the middle of the sea, cutting the sleeping forms at the wrists, drawing blood. They bound each body to a heavy rock—all of them collected from the sacrificial pit, days before. Luka didn't blink, didn't think, didn't spend a tear over his parents, while Andrej and he lowered them into the sea, leaving the rocks to do their thing. His smile didn't waver the whole time, so stuck on his face, it felt frozen. He was probably a ghastly sight, a grin of white teeth visible in the night.

Before they pushed Roko over the boat's rim, Luka punched him in the face for the last time, for good measure.

Moonlight was reflected on the still water, so black they couldn't see a thing under it. They waited calmly. In complete silence, the only warmth they felt came from holding hands. At one point Andrej put his forehead on Luka's, their breaths mingling. So close to a kiss.

A splashing sound alerted them. Four glowing rocks emerged from the depths, breaking the serene surface and the darkness. Green fingers with sharp claws were holding them, an offering. Luka and Andrej complied, taking the stones aboard. Their little vessel was alight in the midst of the black as they rowed back.

In the morning, the rocks stood at Luka's terrace, still glowing slightly, even under the sun. People gathered and stood in front of his house, their eyes open wide. Kate sobbed a sad story, how their parents couldn't live with what they'd done, finally getting into the sea so some other child shouldn't need to be sacrificed so soon after the last one. In her retelling, they'd left Luka and her with a heavy confession.

Her teary tale blew wide open the secret about the early Giving, shocking people, making them feel betrayed and angry. New couples were especially enraged. And while strife continued to rise between families, the rocks were slowly losing their light, day by day, until their glow had dimmed to nothingness. Nobody dared to say anything to them, and Kate almost achieved a saintly status among young parents. Even if some of the old guard, Roko's fishermen buddies, in particular, did squint suspiciously at Luka.

He was unable to stay there. That hadn't changed. And Kate wanted a new life, away from the village, no matter her newfound status. "This marriage, it's a chain for the both of us," she said, urging him to leave. Finally, with a new plan, he kissed his daughter and hugged his wife, promising them money. Knew there was a chance he would not be seeing them again.

He got in the boat with Andrej, letting the sea stretch out the distance between the three of them, until Kate and Luce were nothing but specks on the horizon.

The houses were growing from the seabed, covered in seaweed, urchins, and sea cucumbers. The windows were no more than holes in the rocks, letting the water inside. The houses littered the bottom of the sea, once a mountain above sea level, of which only the peak was now left, protruding from the water. A small island, nothing more, was left from the whole, vast place.

So deep underwater, there was no daylight to break the darkness, only glowing rocks, shining like hundreds of little lamps. Illuminating the sunken village.

Thousands of reflecting eyes showed the hidden bodies behind the house walls, tangled in the weed, merging with the green. Waiting. What for, she didn't know, but the eyes were gathering in the dark, countless, infinite. Bodies floating in the water, bloated, glassy. Dead. The expensive cameras, phones, and bags mingled with their half-eaten corpses. Little green bodies curiously swam in the midst of the trash, collecting it. Making themselves necklaces out of fingerbones.

Ema jolted back to consciousness, the dream drifting from her mind, reflecting eyes turning into golden sparks on her eyelids. She felt every inch of her body, from the soles of her feet to the top of her head. The hurt transcended any possible scale, leaving her body in a state of tingling shock. She felt halfway between fire and exhaustion, deep cuts covering the length of her body. But the tears she could taste on her lips had nothing to do with being in pain, and all with the knowledge she'd failed. Laura's face, while she was submerging, etched in her mind.

"Ema? Ema, wake up," an impossible voice said, hands shaking her. Her eyelids felt stuck, but she forced them open, her head exploding with new, unthinkable pain under the light of the sun. Before she lost consciousness again, her sight fell on the love of her life, Laura's face in a twist of dread.

Her hair a shade of dark green, the color of olives.

Ema had been struck by lightning, while they'd been sleeping in the open, during an unexpected storm. It was the official story they'd been told, even though no one was able to explain the numerous cuts and bites marking Ema's body.

She wasn't aware of the helicopter ride toward the nearest hospital, which was, of course, in a city kilometers away, on the mainland. Laura will later say it was like an action movie with The Rock, trying, but failing, to look all calm and collected while she was sitting at Ema's side on her hospital bed.

The wounds would heal, she was told by the doctors. But the scars would stay forever.

She didn't mind. Given what she'd been on the verge of losing that night, having to live with visible wounds was a small price to pay.

Laura traced the Lichtenberg figures on Ema's skin, starting from her forehead, growing over her left cheek, sliding down the neck, and then blooming wide, like branches on a tree over her chest and stomach. "It's like a sexy, mysterious scar in fiction. You know, like whatever that was on Gerard Butler for the Phantom. I'll have to constantly fight off the ladies and gents vying for your attention."

Ema took Laura's hand in hers. "Too bad for them I'm already taken." Laura sniffed, her eyes watering.

"Maybe you shouldn't be, after what I did. So, so stupid."

"Hey, hey." Ema didn't have a lot of strength right now, but she clenched Laura's arm as hard as she could. Which wasn't much. "It's not your fault. Really." It was further from the truth. It was Ema that surrendered herself to the lightning, a sacrifice willingly made, with a clear mind.

But she couldn't really explain that to Laura, who didn't remember anything from that night, just waking up on the beach and finding Ema's mangled body beside her. Which frightened her to hell and back.

She couldn't even look in the mirror and see the truth of what had happened. Her hair was golden blond to everyone's eyes, except Ema's left one, under the Lichtenberg trail on her eyelid.

At times, Ema would close her left eye, to act like everything was as it used to be for a moment. Like when they were normal. But sometimes, she would close her right, and see the truth for what it was—Laura's hair had turned deep green, her grin showing off the sharp shark's teeth. But, mostly she held both her eyes open, even though it meant Laura's face was constantly shifting in between.

It didn't matter. The only thing that mattered was that she had Laura back, even if a part of her partner, soon-to-be wife, craved raw fish and saltwater, her teeth now capable of drawing blood from every kiss.

Mistress of Geese

Jela froze in place as soon as the evening's peace—during which she was closing the chicken in their coop—was cut short by a sudden gaggling. Geese were never a good sign, especially not those which were currently coming out of the fog at the edge of the forest behind her house, abrupt like hail in summer. A gaggle was spawning from the darkness, marching down the small hill to her yard with purpose. Knowing better than to be caught in the open, Jela rushed to her modest wooden cabin, locked the door behind her, and then put the chair under the doorknob—just in case.

The gaggling was getting louder with every minute, followed by the flutter of a dozen wings. She peeked through the window, her arm at her chest. The muddy ground was lost under the white feathers, just as the thick fog spreading with the geese now covered the view of the chicken coop and the bee hives in the distance. The only color outside her window was the red of the small, marching eyes.

The geese were passing by Jela's house, apparently ignoring her completely. In front of their unstoppable steps, the rusty gate moved with a squeaky sound, opening all on its lonesome to let the gaggle outside. One of the birds, though, stopped, catching Jela's gaze in the window, before separating from the rest. The goose moved towards her, lowering its long neck while simultaneously spreading its wings, the beak slightly opened like the mouth of a snake getting ready to bite its prey. It came all the way to the widow, angry eyes fixed on Jela as if challenging her as if mocking her. Jela shuddered, waiting with her breath stuck to see what the unholy beast would do next, a prayer to the forgotten gods ready on her lips.

The abrupt blow of the head on the glass made Jela flinch in surprise, so much so that she moved away from the window, freaked out. She looked towards the kitchen, her prayer forgotten, ready to dash towards a knife or an ax. But it looked like the goose was done with her because it had already gone back to its place in the foggy white procession outside Jela's home. When the last bird went through the gate, it closed with a heavy whine.

The only thing left behind the gaggle was the fog and the feathers, still falling like snow on the dirty ground.

Jela tried to reason with herself in every way conceivable that this was not her problem, no way. If her Mistress decided to let her minions loose on the world, who was Jela to stop them or turn them back? She had not signed up for this. But the image of fiery crimson eyes, looking at her through the window, kept bugging her. The geese usually didn't come out of the woods for no reason. What if she was supposed to follow them?

Ignoring the unease, she came to the simple conclusion that, if her Mistress expected something specific from Jela, she should've sent her a clearer message than the gaggle.

Jela didn't need to wait for too long for a more direct order, though, and she soon regretted not following the geese immediately. The morning after the birds' visit, the first thing that suffered were the unpicked apples in her orchard, having simply rotted away on the branches during the night. With the first rays of the muted sun, trying so hard to pass through the fog, Jela found the putrid fruit shrouding the ground in black.

She didn't even have the time to clean up the mess, when her chickens started dropping one by one, struck dead by a sudden plague. The last hit, though, was when she learned that all of her little bees had perished away. It was that final thing—the image of their tiny, still bodies—to cut her from below and manage to bring her to tears she thought she didn't have anymore.

"Alright! Message received, loud and clear!" she shouted at the air, in the direction of the forest on the hill behind her cottage. "I'll go after the stupid birds, although, you know, you could've just sent me a paper with instructions," she whispered under her breath, even though she knew her Mistress will hear her no matter how quietly she spoke.

Mumbling curses, she pulled dusty clothes reeking of mothballs, but decent enough to be seen in public out of the closet; tied up her long, tangled hair in a ponytail, and went out into the village, after the geese.

Everywhere she looked, the landscape was so still and calm that the act of moving felt unnerving. Jela sloshed through the wet mud in her brown boots, keeping an eye on the fallen feathers from yesterday.

She passed by tall sunflowers—turned towards each other rather than the sky—bright red apples on the trees, gaping yards, empty pumpkin fields, cornfields, and vineyards. There wasn't a living soul in sight, nor a tractor on the road. The only things that she could hear were her own steps and the rustling of corn leaves in the wind. She walked like that, her fists deep in the pocket, following her white feathery trail towards the town of Lepoglava, until, in the distance, she saw a barricade on the road, a police car, close to the entrance of the town she was approaching.

Unwilling to deal with the police, she turned off the road and into the fields, risking the homeowners' anger rather than having any sort of interaction with the so-called mundane authority. But she didn't need to worry. Just like the village that she'd passed, it looked like the entirety of Lepoglava was closed off in their homes. Or, almost.

One man was standing outside, butchering chicken at the stump, when Jela stumbled upon his yard. Blood splattered through the open wound of the chicken's neck, body convulsing in the air. Tiny drops landed all over the man's plaid shirt, soaked the ground, and washed over his black rubber boots. However, what surprised Jela was the deer-in-the-headlights look in his eyes when he saw her as if she'd caught him doing something bad. She raised her hand in a wave, but, instead of an answer, the man appeared so enraged that, for a moment, she feared he might pounce on her with the ax he gripped tightly with his hand. A few heartbeats passed, during which only the dripping of blood could be heard, and then the man turned around and hastily retreated to his house, pushing the knob with his elbow since he was not letting go of either the slaughtered chicken or the ax.

Confused, Jela continued on.

As she got back to the main road, now well worried, she decided to leave her trail for a moment and try and look for someone who could explain to her what was going on. She had a feeling that this geese's quest from her Mistress and the deathly village peace might be connected. But every bar turned out to be closed, all cars parked, and there was no one else outside, not even a stray.

If not for that man and the police car, she would've thought she'd come to a dead town.

She was contemplating whether she should try and knock on some doors, just to assure herself that there are still living people there, when she found a Konzum, calling to her with its opened door.

Two cashiers were inside; welcoming her like specters with white medical masks on their faces and rubber gloves on their hands. It was true that years had passed since Jela had last been among people, but she was pretty sure this wasn't supposed to be some fashion statement. Two pairs of eyes above the masks followed her entrance with suspicion and a bit of annoyance as if she'd broken into their homes. Jela's greeting went unanswered, but they didn't forbid her to enter the grocery store, so she went inside and went deeper among the empty shelves. *That* fascinated her the most. Never in her life had she seen that kind of emptiness in a store. Looking at price tags, it appeared that the stuff which was the scarcest was flour, wet wipes, toilet paper, and wine. Jela wasn't really certain what she was looking for, other than, maybe, some newspaper to check if there was an explanation for this strange behavior, since both of the cashiers were too hostile for an attempt at chatting.

Aimlessly, she almost crashed into a little old lady, her hair hidden under the tight red scarf, who was having trouble with pushing her half-filled cart, wheezing along.

The granny looked at her and raised her eyebrows in surprise.

"Are you alright, Grandmother? Do you need any help?" Out of a corner of her eye, among the shelves, Jela saw one of the cashiers, who was watching them closely.

The old woman coughed into her shawl and signaled with her hand for Jela to move away from her. "There's not a lot of people coming near those who cough these days," the elder answered a question Jela didn't even ask. "That means you're either arrogant or without fear."

Jela shrugged. "Or maybe I was just being polite, brought up to help—" she almost added *the weak*, but thought better of it "—those in need. But why should I be afraid?"

For a moment, the old woman looked too astonished to reply, but then she started laughing so hard that her laughter quickly turned into a coughing fit. At the edge of their aisle, there wasn't just one cashier anymore. Now both of them were standing there, openly watching, like predators.

"Because of the sickness, dear child, where have you been these last few days? Have you crawled out of some cave? They say that kids these days are glued to their screens; is it possible you have no idea what's happening?"

Jela couldn't explain—nor did she have time for that—her life situation to the strange granny at the grocery store. Why she's not in the possession of television, radio, or internet, to stay in the loop with the world outside her little wooden home. Or why she had no visitors who could gossip about the news.

"I'm isolated," she said in the end. "This is the first time I came to the town after many years. Trauma," she added as a simple, unsolicited explanation. "I'm afraid I'm not well informed."

"Then I'll inform you, dear child. A terrible disease appeared. No one knows where from, but they say it started in our town. It's spreading fast, too fast, in fact, and everyone who catches it lies down with a fever and a cough so violent it feels like you're losing your lungs." As if she wanted to prove her point, the old woman shuddered with another strong burst of coughing. "Some say that there are those who fall in a sleep so deep no one can rouse them from it. Some even found their death in their dreams. The whole city is quarantined. Maybe even the whole country. Only this store is open, so people have something to eat, as well as the pharmacy. The sick are afraid to fall asleep, because they don't know if they'll be able to ever wake again. The healthy are afraid to go outside, so they don't fall ill. Is it possible you didn't hear anything about this, dear sun?"

Jela shook her head no. Were geese guilty for this disease? But why would her Mistress let them loose on the people to saw seeds of plague, only to send Jela after them to get them back in the woods? It didn't make much sense. And too little time had passed for the gaggle to do this much damage.

Granny suddenly leaned over the basket, choking on her own cough.

"Oh for... what's enough is enough. Out with you! Right now!" one of the cashiers shrieked at the old woman in pain.

"Out with you both, until you infect us! Do you want us all to die, assholes?" the other one joined in. That one even had a broom in her hand, brandishing it like a sword. Ready to beat them to submission if needed.

Not caring much for the old woman's warning, Jela took her frail body under her arm. At the same moment, she smelled a strong odor wafting from the woman's hair, but she didn't show discomfort. It wouldn't be polite. "Come, Grandmother, let me help you get home."

The elderly woman was surprised, but she let Jela touch her. Arm in arm, they left the store and the groceries that cashiers didn't even let them buy.

"You're a strange one," the granny told her in the end.

It didn't take long for them to get to the old woman's home, a small, single storey house, although she kept coughing throughout the whole short journey. She coughed so much that, a few times, they had to stop to wait out her great shivering. All the while, Jela tried very hard to ignore the stench from the woman's hair, thinking she probably didn't have the strength to wash it. It was only when she helped the little old lady enter her kitchen—strongly smelling of human meat—that Jela finally started to suspect whom she was following home. The woman watched her with arched eyebrows as she sat at the round table, while Jela, trusting her instincts, opened the fridge door.

In the fridge, on the shelves, she found the neatly arranged remains of a child.

After closing the doors, she turned toward the old woman.

"Don't worry, it wouldn't be polite to kill you and eat you now, after you've helped me," the old woman said, misinterpreting Jela's look.

Jela herself wasn't sure how to feel. She'd figured out long ago that there wasn't any sadness left in her for the dead. Rationally, she knew she should mourn the loss of a child's life, but all of her emotions were locked behind doors in her soul, and she didn't have the keys.

"Although, I could say I've already killed you by letting you get so near me when I'm so sick."

"The disease doesn't concern me," Jela replied, coming closer to the old woman. The hair's stench. The red scarf. It was so easy to explain everything away. But she knew the stories well and, if she was right, this old scarf was hiding the woman's life. It would be so easy to come close to this old, sick fairy, and tear off the scarf from her hair, stealing her powers away. But Jela wasn't a vengeful person and this fairy was already dying.

"Everyone can get sick, including a fairy like me. Or whatever the hell you are, because human you obviously aren't."

Jela smiled sadly upon hearing that. "I would say that even fairies can get sick when the years catch up to them. You are far away from Kitež-mountain, aren't you, Grandmother?"

The old woman roared with laughter, while large tears started falling from her eyes. "Far away, hundreds of years away."

Jela put her arm on the woman's shoulder as if she were giving her a blessing or forgiveness. In actuality, it was a promise. Everybody has to die one day, even fairies, just like the children they ate. "Take care,

Grandmother. This cough of yours sounds terrible."

"You too, dear child. This sickness, it's not from this world. It's some horrible curse. And if someone doesn't find a way to break it, the whole world could forever fall asleep in an eternal dream."

"So that means I need to kiss someone?" Jela joked. The old woman grinned, showing off her sharp teeth.

"Or kill the one who's cursed us and eat all the meat from their bones. That's my advice. That way, you don't need to worry about whether you've kissed the right person or not."

After leaving the sick fairy in her house, Jela returned to her quest, trying to find the trail of white feathers again. While she was passing through the town, curtains at a window would sometimes move just a bit, hiding the looks that followed her track, and she could even hear dogs barking from some houses. But, save from herself, the streets were still completely empty.

She passed near the prison, gargantuan in its stature like a sleeping giant, and briefly wondered—how did the people in there deal with the sickness? Were all of the guards already sick, leaving the inmates to die of hunger and thirst, abandoned? She didn't have time to find out, so she left the colossus behind her back. Her gaze fixed on the muddy road, she followed the feathers up until the point she finally found the gaggle.

The geese in question were waiting, motionless, in a yard, their red eyes focused straight on the doors of the house that otherwise didn't stand out from the background which Jela already walked through for hours. It was built in the shape of any other house typical for Zagorje, with a big empty yard and an even bigger cornfield.

But the gaggle stood in front of her with their elongated necks, patiently waiting for something only they knew, like a death watch. As soon as they'd heard Jela approaching them, a few of the birds turned their heads towards her, gaggling. Their screams disturbed the day's eerie silence, cutting through the peace with the piercing, throaty *ga ga ga* from the whole standing troop.

She approached the geese and took her hands from her pockets, clenching her fists. The geese didn't move from her path. They wouldn't listen to her if she asked them to give her space. There was no other way to get into the house. Saying a short prayer, Jela straightened her spine out to her full height, and with the confidence she lacked, took a step into the midst of the gaggle.

A rain of beaks instantly started falling all over Jela, trying to find skin through her clothes, any possible piece of her body that they could bite. Otherwise, they let her pass, their bites mostly a warning instead of a real wish to hurt her; a vicious reminder that she was a lower species and that they'd shown her mercy by letting her stay in one piece. Pain followed behind the pinches, the first thing that she truly felt after a long time.

The doors of the house were unlocked. As soon as she entered, the geese started pushing at her back, driving her to move faster. She glanced behind, seeing them twitching their heads left and right as if they were sniffing the air. As if they were looking for something.

Or someone.

One goose was faster than the others, passing Jela and climbing the stairs in quick steps. Knowing the bird was showing her the path, Jela followed it, checking the closed doors by sight only, wondering where the homeowners were.

Upstairs, the only thing she could hear—except for the clock ticking—was the deadly coughing. The closest door stood ajar, so she saw the elderly couple, sleeping in their bed. They weren't dead yet, but she could feel their lives were hanging at a delicate balance, ready to pass away at any moment. The coughing sounded again, and it appeared that the gaggle was going straight to its source.

Opposite the stairs, at the end of the hallway, another door stood, open like the jaws of a Venus flytrap luring the fly. Through the gap, Jela could see a terrace door, a television mounted on a wall and a small cabinet. That was the only room that showed any proof of life, and the geese were disappearing inside, one by one. Knowing she had no other choice but to follow, Jela took a deep breath, clenched her fists, and set off after their sauntering bodies.

Inside, she stumbled upon a vision she hadn't expected.

In the spacious bedroom with washed-out yellow walls, in the huge bed at the window, lying under the heavy quilt made of geese feathers, was a young woman. And under her bed, a gaggle of Jela's Mistress' gathered, spreading their wings and hissing their warnings at the girl. But they didn't dare attack as if they were afraid to come closer to the dying girl.

Jela managed to get through their rows and approach the woman on the bed, slightly nervous.

Thin sun rays fell on the girl's sickly, rosy cheeks and watery eyes. She squinted towards Jela, then blinked in fear, but it appeared as if she couldn't see the geese at all.

"Who... who are you? What are you doing here?" the girl coughed the words, more than saying them.

Jela raised her hand, palm up, hoping that the girl's eyes, springtime forest green, would be able to see that her intentions were good.

"Don't be afraid, I mean you no harm." She knew it didn't sound promising. She did trespass by entering the house. But, for whatever reason, a small smile found its place on the girl's face; calming like chamomile tea on an upset stomach.

"Then you're some sort of an angel. You came to take me because I'm dying. Isn't it right?"

Pain, as if someone had run a blade over her heart, uncomfortably stung in Jela's chest.

"I'm not an angel, far from that," Jela said with a sad smile. Awkwardly, she sat at the edge of the bed, ready to bolt if it seemed like her presence irked the girl. But the young woman smiled and then coughed, again.

"Really? That pretty you could only be an angel. I'm probably hallucinating. I've been alone for so long..."

Jela almost laughed out loud when she heard the compliment, knowing fully well that she looked like a dried-out reed. But she didn't want to contradict the person whose perception was obviously affected by disease and loneliness.

"Yes, you're hallucinating," Jela decided to join in the game, "and this particular hallucination wants to know whether you have any knowledge about what's happening outside? Right now? With this sickness?"

The woman blinked, her eyelids closing down more and more. For a moment, it looked like she would fall asleep, but she managed to open her eyes with great pain and focus on Jela.

"This hallucination is rude because she didn't even introduce herself. What's your name? You look like a flower. Violet, maybe?"

"Jela, actually."

"Oh, so I was close. A tree, not a flower. Evergreen, eternal. Surely, you're not going to die of this sickness. My name is Rose, and everyone knows roses wither with time."

The young woman, Rose, started to cry quietly—small drops trickling down her round cheeks.

"And firs die too," Jela said, in hope that it will cheer the girl up. But she started to cry even harder hearing that.

"You shouldn't be here. If you're not already sick, you'll surely catch it now. And there's nothing valuable here to steal."

Jela's heart hurt. Not only was the girl in front of her in obvious agony, but she also believed Jela to be a thief—and yet she worried about Jela's health, more than what Jela planned to do to *her*. Thinking about what to say, she decided to take a risk and try the truth.

"I can't get sick," Jela calmly said. "For that to be possible, I'd need to be alive, first."

Rose's eyes were full of surprise under the bushy brows, searching for the truth in Jela's face.

"If you're not alive, and you're not an angel, what are you?" It was the inevitable question, one that Jela expected. She sighed, but since she'd opened that can of worms, she could very well explain it.

"I was alive once, just like you. And now I'm more of a... lighthouse keeper. Except I'm not in a lighthouse, it's more like..." She was trying to find the words to explain what she'd become after her death. What her solemn duty was. "I'm like a guard for the underworld's gate." Jela saw the crucifix upon the girl's bed and went with that analogy. "Hell's gate. That's not entirely correct. It's not a door as much as it is a forest and, besides that, Hell is a Christian thing. But it's closest to the truth."

Rose's face was blank, without a hint whether she believed Jela or not. But it looked like she was mulling after Jela's words. In the end, maybe she'd decide this was all a hallucination of her tormented mind.

"The gate of Hell is in Zagorje?" she finally said, with humor in her eyes and voice.

"The underworld's gates are all over the world. And new ones are constantly popping up." Jela wasn't sure what had overcome her senses, to be so candid with the dying girl, but she couldn't stop. She would jump in the middle of the gaggle waiting behind her back, let them peck the meat from her bones, before denying something to Rose. A familiar emotion started creeping up unexpectedly, although she'd believed that she'd never be able to feel anything real. An emotion that came in the most inopportune moments.

It wasn't fair that she could remember life, when she'd already lost hers.

"And how do you become a guard of said doors?" Rose asked, curiously. But, she probably saw how Jela blanched upon her words because she rushed to add, without waiting for Jela's answer: "You don't need to tell me, I apologize, I wasn't thinking, it must be something truly personal to—"

"No, no, it's alright," Jela interrupted, with a forced smile. "Well, in my case, you become a guard when someone very close to you, whom you'd loved very dearly, dies. So you do something stupid, something as arrogant as making a deal with Death. If you win the game against Death, the loved one will get back to you, back among the living. But if you fail... well, then you stay away with the dead, working for Death."

"I've, obviously, lost. On the bright side, I don't have to worry about ever being unemployed again, but on the other... well, you know. Death. If nothing else, I never felt the moment I died. It didn't hurt, it wasn't dramatic, or anything like that. I just... fell asleep. And when I woke up, I wasn't at home anymore. I wasn't even alive anymore."

Even though she hasn't been dead for a long time, only a dozen years or so, it was harder and harder to recollect the life she'd led before her untimely death. Once she lost the game, her life didn't pass before her eyes. She just closed them and everything suddenly disappeared. The only thing she remembered nowadays was that burning will and a belief, strong as the Sun, that knew no limits; she'd believed her love was stronger than the world, as indestructible as a rock. She forgot that even mountains could fall. That nothing was eternal or certain, except death.

"Is all death like that? Peaceful, like dreaming?" the girl asked, probably for her own sake. Jela didn't like that at all. She put her palm on Rose's cheek. The girl was burning like a bonfire lit for Midsummer's Eve.

"Listen to me well. You're not going to die. You'll

live for a very long time." The words stung her tongue, making her fear she was promising something she wouldn't be able to fulfill.

The girl just sadly smiled at that, obviously not believing it. Jela couldn't resent her for it. She wouldn't, either.

"But to help you, I first need you to help me with something. Okay? You need to answer a few questions."

Rose nodded her head, her eyelids heavy. Jela cursed herself for being so talkative. The last thing she needed was for the girl to fall asleep before she managed to extract important information from her. "Just tell me one more thing, please," Rose begged and Jela already knew she wouldn't have it in her to refuse the girl's wish, no matter that time kept getting away from them. "That person you lost? Do you see them now, when you're working for Death?"

Jela's throat clenched as if someone had tightened a noose around her neck.

"No. When you guard the doors, you don't see what's behind them."

One solitary tear fell from Rose's eye. "That's so sad."

"A lot of years passed." Not so many, but enough to feel like a whole eternity has passed, the days looking exactly the same, with little change. "I cried over my fate long ago; now I'm just an employee, like any other," she joked, hoping to lighten the atmosphere. As easy as Sisyphus' task. With Rose's disease and mentions of Jela's death, a cadaverous weight fell over the room.

"My turn." Jela decided it was time to get back at the business at hand. "The sickness. How did it start?"

"It was just a common cold." Tears started to swell in the green eyes, but Rose's voice was calm and she continued without a hitch. "Or so I thought. I didn't have a reason to think anything else might've been amiss. I did everything as I normally would. Even though I felt sick, I didn't stop, thinking it was just a cold all the time. But then my parents got sick too."

"Then our relatives, and my friends. And soon, everyone else. When my condition got worse, it was already too late. My parents were so sick they couldn't drive me to the nearby hospital, and since it was already quarantined, I thought, it was better to stay home anyway. Only, we're all so sick now that none of us can get out of bed. I don't even know... I don't even know if my parents... are still alive... I don't know when was the last time I saw them... the last time I ate."

Tears started trickling down the rosy cheeks and Jela tried to dry them with her palms. Gently, she wiped Rose's face, visibly calming her with touch.

"Someone's cursed you very badly, Rose." Jela agreed with the old fairy. There was no other explanation. Jela's Mistress wouldn't have let her beloved gaggle out in the world if this disease had been natural.

"Pardon?"

Jela tried to explain the best she could. Someone, as it appeared, wanted great harm to befall Rose, so they tried to curse her, to make her fall ill or even, maybe, dead, but something had gone wrong because the sickness didn't stop with her, becoming contagious instead. Like a domino effect, others got sick, too.

"It's my fault?" Rose asked in the end. "For everything? I—"

"No," Jela interrupted her again before the girl could slip into an abyss from which it would be hard to come out. "The only guilty party in this whole story is the person who cursed you. Okay? Do you know anyone who might have a grudge against you? Someone who's jealous, or angry at you for something?"

"I don't know, I don't know, who could hate me so much to curse me?" Rose muttered through hysterical laughter and a cough. But then, suddenly, she stilled. "Maybe... There's this guy. I... we used to be close friends, and he read too much into it. When I rejected his advances, he was furious. He said that I'll come to regret it. I thought he was going to spread some nasty rumor about me, or, worst-case scenario—which I feared the most, I confess—that he was going to greet me with an ax one day. But curse? Do you really think, that's—"

"Yes." She didn't need to think too much nor investigate. Sometimes, the real answer was the most obvious one.

"But how?"

Jela shrugged. *How* wasn't the question they should concern themselves with.

"Maybe he's a *mogut*. Or he knows someone with a real *power*. In any case, I doubt he knew the disease would spread like this. But that's not important right now." Jela turned to look at the geese which were watching the two of them closely, eyes bright red like Hell's door.

She knew what to do to break the curse and banish the sickness from this world.

"Rose, I need his name."

"Wait!" An arm came up from under the quilt and

caught Jela's palm that was still caressing Rose's cheek. For someone who was deadly sick, she had an iron grip. Jela froze, unsure what to expect from the girl—as if she'd suddenly transformed into a siren who's planning to drag her under the surface and drown her in a deep blue sea. "Whatever you plan to do... if it succeeds. If I recover. Will I ever see you again? Because it would be terribly heartbreaking if our first meeting was also our last."

Jela almost choked on her own spit so she tried to turn it into laughter.

"Be careful what you speak, someone would think you were flirting while you're on your deathbed."

"Isn't that the best time to flirt?" Rose joked. Her eyes fluttered, fighting against the sleep, but it was only a matter of time before she finally slipped into a dream. Jela wasn't sure if she could count on ever getting her back if that happened. So she responded with a strong grip of a sweaty palm and said something completely out of her mind:

"When you get better, we'll talk again, you'll see. Maybe we could even have dinner." It was a promise she couldn't keep, but she didn't want to break the heart of a girl who's already lost everything else. "But for that to happen, you need to give me a *name*."

Finally contented, Rose lowered her head on her pillow and whispered a name like a vow which sealed their deal.

Jela found herself standing before yet another house which would usually look inconspicuous except for a special brand of tension spreading out of it, like smoke from a chimney. It felt like time had stopped moving, with the house frozen in a photograph she was now walking all over in her muddy boots. Following after Jela, the gaggle was not far behind; standing at attention, their elongated necks lowered, their wings half spread.

"I know you're in there!" she shouted at the house when her knocking went unanswered. She saw, though, a slight movement behind the curtain at the second storey window—a surefire sign of life hiding behind closed doors.

"I only need Ivek! Others can stay inside! If he doesn't come out, I can't promise safety to others!" There was no sign that anybody had heard her. No one showed up at the window to curse her or to try to chase her away with an air rifle, though. Maybe they'd mistaken her for a mad woman shouting at the sky. Or maybe they knew quite well why she was there and were cautious enough not to open the doors. Ivek probably knew what had become of his petty revenge.

She sat on the ground, legs crossed.

"I'm not going anywhere!" she yelled at the brick and plaster again, the house completely silent before her. "I'm not going away until Ivek comes out and faces me!"

She stayed like that, yelling, for three whole hours. Nobody came out of the house. Nobody tried to chase her away from their yard. The only movement from the house was a shudder from the curtain like someone had come to check if she was still there. When the last sun rays retreated behind the hill, she decided enough time had passed.

She approached the old doors and placed her hand on the doorknob. The doors were locked, but she didn't expect anything less.

Jela closed her eyes and whispered an invocation to her Mistress. When she pushed down, there was no resistance. She opened the door as if it had been unlocked the whole time.

Death could pass anywhere and no doors—neither metal nor plastic nor wooden nor golden—could stop her.

Behind her back, the geese opened their beaks and let out a gut-churning scream, audible from Hell and back. Jela moved out of their way and let the gaggle in the house.

She sat under the window instead, stretching her legs. A collection of sounds could be heard from the house—fluttering of wings, gaggling, running, furniture and glass smashing, and, worst of all—people and children screaming. Jela started singing under her breath, just to distract herself from the sounds of the massacre—the only thing that managed to escape outside the door. She'd told them to send Ivek to her. Warned them it was the only thing that could've saved the lot of them.

Jela closed her eyes and tried to imagine what Rose looked like when she was healthy. The things she did in her everyday life. Did she love reading or watching movies? Did she help in the fields or was she more of a city kid? She tried to imagine the sound of her voice when it wasn't riddled with coughing. How green her eyes might be when they weren't drowned in fever. She let her imagination run wild—envisioning a possibility of them seeing each other again after Rose had recovered. A world in which they could sit at the same table and share a pie made from Jela's apples. At that moment, she allowed herself—while the sensation of strangers dying warmed her back, leaning against the house as she was—to believe this day was not the only one they could have in this place and time.

A few moments passed before she finally realized there was a single tear sliding down her cheek. She wasn't certain whether she was crying for the senseless deaths behind her, or for herself. She didn't like it either way. She'd made peace with her fate and it wasn't fair someone could destroy her peace of mind like this. And yet, one tear managed to sneak out, leaving a bitter taste in its wake.

She wasn't certain how much time had passed, but the moon showed up in the night sky when the first geese started exiting the house, covered in red, with no hints of a white feather, drenched in blood; dripping while they moved. Some of them still had meat stuck in their beaks and bits of tissue and innards they were slurping in pleasure. Jela peeked inside the house through the opened door, catching only traces of a struggle—bloody goose prints, walls splattered with crimson, floors covered with white, gnawed-out bones, some of which still had some little bits of flesh on them—and decided she didn't need to know in full what had happened in the house.

How many souls had been there? How many kids? How many old people?

They should've let Ivek out.

And nothing would've happened to them. This way, it was impossible to distinguish Ivek's remains from the others.

Jela got back to her home, numb inside, feeling nothing but the chill in her bones. She opened the gate to her yard and let the geese saunter back to the woods on top of the hill; with full stomachs and pleased. As the geese moved, so did the worst of the omnipresent fog—following them into the forest. One goose pinched her while passing by, but it didn't hurt as the earlier bites did. It was almost gentle, like it was thanking her for a feast.

It didn't take long for Jela to figure out she could hear chickens clucking, as well as the buzzing of a living hive. Everything she'd left dead, now welcomed her alive. The apple trees bore new fruit. The bee hives hummed with life and work. Chickens spread around her, pecking corn from the ground. Two of the chicks found a piece of an intestine—which had probably fallen from a goose's beak—and started to fight over who gets to eat it.

Jela's Mistress was sometimes cruel, but she also took care of her.

Her eyes watered. She sat on a stump and watched chickens fight over human remains.

A sound at the gate distracted Jela from wood chopping. Warmth wasn't a thing she still needed, just like food, but that didn't mean she didn't enjoy both of them. And the weather had started getting colder with the days, the air smelling of snow.

Surprised because, of course, there was no one to visit her, nor anyone who knew where to find her, Jela raised her gaze from the logs and froze upon seeing the vision at her gate.

There, in a white coat and a crimson shawl, stood Rose. Sunlight was caught in her hair and her bright smile. Rose raised a hand and waved. In the other, she carried a wicker basket.

Doubting her eyes, ready for the girl to be a specter, Jela lowered the ax near the stump and approached the iron door with unsteady steps.

"Hey, hello, I wasn't sure if I'll be able to find you. That is, I wasn't sure that it would really lead me to you, but, lo and behold, it did," the girl babbled, her voice vibrant, completely healthy. No idea what to say in response, Jela stood there, opening and closing her mouth, like a fish on land. She was close enough to reach out through the bars and touch the girl, or open the gates, but she didn't do either, still too much in shock.

"How did you find me?" Up until this point, she wasn't certain anyone could do that. Obviously, someone could, because what was the point of her guarding the gates of the underworld in Zagorje, if there was no one who would try to enter? But, so far, every villager had passed her house as if it didn't even exist.

"I found these white feathers everywhere on the road. And I had a feeling, if I followed them, they'll bring me to you. Somehow, I had this recurring dream in which a whole gaggle stood behind you while we talked, looking at me with evil eyes, spawned from Hell. I would wake up covered in sweat, gripped with fear, like waking from a horrible nightmare. But something nudged me to start following the trail of feathers. I thought I'd end up looking like some deranged Gretel, except it looks like I was right. I did find you."

This wasn't a coincidence. Not the part that there were leftover feathers, nor the part that Rose could see them while awake, nor the gut feeling that it was a trail left for her to find Jela.

Jela's Mistress could really be cruel sometimes.

She gripped the iron bars, hard.

"Why did you come here?" Her question sounded too harsh, too dismissive, and Rose flinched. Her bright sunny smile slipped from her face. At the same time, Jela felt like the worst monster that could crawl out from the forest behind her house.

"I wanted to thank you," the other woman said demurely, suddenly insecure. "My parents too, they managed to pull through. The disease disappeared." She didn't say anything about Ivek or his family. Jela didn't ask.

"I wasn't sure what a Hell gates guard ate, but I reckoned I couldn't go wrong with chocolate," she started babbling again, pointing at the whisker basket in her hand. "And cakes. And wine. The good kind! Not from Zagorje, of course."

Jela couldn't help herself. A smile escaped into her stern face and as soon as the girl saw it, her own came back, shining brighter than the summer sun. Jela could even feel its warmth.

"Thank you, although you didn't need to bring me anything. It was just a job." She regretted her words as soon as Rose saddened upon hearing that. Like a kicked puppy, she lowered her eyes to the ground.

"It didn't feel like *just a job*, while we were talking. I thought..." The sentence broke off, lingering in the air with all the possible endings. Jela could catch any one which would make the most sense, remind the other girl that she shouldn't mix up with the dead when there were so many living souls still in the world; she could be cruel enough to show her that Jela herself was nothing but a monster to hide from.

Instead of all of that, she reached with her hand through the gates and touched Rose's face, lifting her chin. She was warm and soft, like flowers blooming in spring.

"You can't enter the woods. That's the only thing forbidden here. That's the only thing you'll promise me. Then, and only then, I'll let you inside and we can share the cakes you brought me."

Rose almost squealed with happiness and Jela hoped she didn't just make the worst mistake of her posthumous life.

She opened the gate and let the sun break through the eternal fog of the yard.

The Sound of Wind

ALL OF THE SOUNDS stopped for a moment when a mother's cry cut through the quiet ringing of bells as if the goats, sheep, and cows could feel the heavy blanket of fear, freezing everyone in that moment. Little Ivica, who had, just like other kids, gotten up that day and gone to school on foot, in the silence of the black woods, never came to the small white building which sat in the looming mountain's lap. Nor did he come back home—and it was only when the others returned that people learned that something was amiss.

Ivica had split up from the other kids, it would appear. The group of them, with their small bundles and battered-up clothes, braved the woods in the early hours every day, to break through the thick fir forest to the school closest to their village, still miles away. But that morning strife had happened—something unimportantly small and petulant—which had ended in one bloody nose and one missing kid.

Woodsmen, shepherds and hunters—a scrambled group from all neighboring villages, slight in numbers as they were after they'd recently fought in the Second World War—went into the forest to search for him, shouting his name all the way, while the women tried to console his despairing mother. After all, if nothing had happened, he should've found his way to the school or back home, having walked through those woods ever since his first steps. But the more time passed, the more it became obvious that little Ivica wasn't coming back.

Wolves or bears, it was proclaimed to the teary mother, spoken with utmost confidence. Instead of the boy, hunters came back with a slaughtered wolf, promptly skinned at the village center, the skin presented to the grieving parent as a trophy, still dripping with warm blood. The head was mounted on a stake, its bulging eyes and lolling tongue a cautionary tale for the remaining kids. *See what lives in the woods. If you're not careful, you'll end up just like that, ripped apart among the wolves.*

And life continued as if nothing had happened. The sun came up and down over the thick, whispering forest surrounding the small village, settled in a valley deep underneath the steep mountain slope, connected to the other six nearby villages only by small mountain roads more suitable for the goats.

Bura tried to ignore the evil looks which were following her around the village. Holding her head high, refusing to slouch, as Granny had taught her, she walked over to the village center and grabbed water from the deep well. The mumbled gossip and squinty eyes turned towards her still managed to get under her skin, turning into an ache she could never heal with herbs, no matter how hard she tried to tell herself that it didn't matter. That she didn't care.

It never stopped hurting.

There was a woman near the well, but she wasn't interested in the water. It was Aunt Ika, her body gaunt, arms so thin they looked like sticks, as easily broken. Her muddled eyes wandered over the village, without a clear focus, clasping at the wolf pelt she wore like a cape, draped tight around the chest.

She was bemoaning something to herself, always talking to an invisible audience. She will stroll around like this until her husband comes home from pasture, and forces her into their house, away from the prying eyes.

Bura turned her gaze away. Her self-pity had been replaced with pity for someone else.

After filling the wooden bucket, circled with hoops made from ash branches, she put it on her back, glad that there was enough water again in the village thanks to the rain, after the long drought in the summer heat. Just remembering the summer made her back and legs hurt with phantom burns. Even when they had every right to their water ration, it appeared their share was always smaller, no matter that the village elders who guarded the well would never admit that. So it meant a long day's journey for Bura. Now, though, she only needed to survive a brief outing in the village.

"It needs blood," a sudden, intelligible sentence directed at her made Bura stop in her tracks. It was Aunt Ika, now looking right at her with an eerie focus that wasn't usually there. While Bura was grasping at the water bucket, the other woman approached her, her knuckles white from clutching the pelt at her heart. "Again and again, it's always hungry for more. Dilonoga knew that. He knew. We forgot."

Bura didn't know what to say, so she stayed silent, glimpsing over Ika's shoulder to see if there was anyone who could take the woman off her hands. Everyone who had watched her descent into the village had suddenly lost interest and was doing something else.

"We should give *you* this time." Ika's eyes—abruptly

clear as if they had never been clouded over—looked directly at Bura, so there was no mistaking whom her words had been intended for. "It should've taken you the first time too, not my sweet boy."

Bura took a deep breath, her hands shaking with rage. The woman was mumbling nonsense, but the message was loud and clear. Before Ika could say anything else to her, Bura turned on her heels and fled.

The air was filled with slight jingles of bells at the cattle's necks, dog barks and the shepherds' whooping song and quips after getting back from the pasture. High mountain tops devoured the sun earlier each day, so they all had to come back sooner than the day before, or they would risk getting caught in the woods at dusk. As the sun sunk behind the sharp white stone, it cast longer shadows over the village, and other people only got blurrier to Bura's eyes, dark elongated forms made of contempt and foul words. One of the figures, whom she recognized as a woodsman known in their village only as Nuncle—no matter the familial connections—was sitting in front of his house, with an air of not one care in the world, except for the ax he still had, now loosely leaning on his leg. As an afterthought. Pipe smoke coiled in the air with his exhale, obscuring his face, but she could still feel his gaze burning holes in her head. She shouldn't fear him, or Ika, or anyone else, yet she still rushed towards her shabby wooden home at the edge of the village, where the firs and the spruce trees encroached on their land, as much as she could with her precious weight.

Hoping no one would see it fit to cross over her path. The loud laughter of shepherds at her heels, kindling a fire under her steps, the jingle ominously setting up a fast pace.

"Look at you, fast as the wind. You'll hurt yourself," Granny's voice welcomed her as soon as she burst into the house, like the devils were at her feet.

"Sun's setting," she simply said, hoping Granny will misunderstand her rosy cheeks for fast walking, not fearful shame.

Bura put the bucket on its designated bench and straightened her back, her muscles stretching and untangling. Slight pops of her joints mingled with the crackling of the fire. The comforting smell of warm milk, wool, and cow manure embraced her like loving arms, in Granny's place, who was sitting by the open hearth, carving something out of a piece of wood. Most of the people in the village used stoves these days. Not her Granny, though, who preferred the old hearth which had been there from the time the house was built—more than fifty years ago. In the same way, Granny was against setting up electricity in the house, even if they had the opportunity and money to do it, which they did not.

Bura closed the few chickens they had in the coop before checking up on Bela, the skinny white cow with bulging black eyes, who was munching on the hay in the cellar, while her tail sailed through the air, landing on flies at her back. She was quite old but, fortunately, still gave milk. Bura put her hand on Bela's neck, looking deeply into those empty eyes.

"Just one more winter, please," she begged the cow, begged God. Bura didn't know what she'd do when, one day, she descended the stairs to milk the cow, only to end up with a dry bucket between her knees. Or, even worse, to find Bela dead. "One more winter." It was easy to say. It wasn't like next year they'd have money for new cattle.

She still prayed. Clenching her fist on the cow's neck, her teeth almost hurting how much she gritted them.

A harsh coughing sound interrupted her morose thoughts, reminding her of another plight. She had to close her eyes for a moment, counting her own breaths, waiting for Granny's coughs to subdue. Granny's coughs were getting worse, and Bura's skin broke out in goosebumps, feeling the cold. It would appear she'll need to add another person to her prayers.

Getting back to the hearth, she took a woolen blanket from the wall shelf and tried to cover Granny, still hunched over her woodcarving.

"Leave me be, I don't need it." The old woman flinched from her, observing the blanket in her arms with the greatest of offense.

"Granny, please," she implored, but her grandma wasn't having it.

"It's not that cold. I know I'm old, but these bones saw through tougher winters than this mellow autumn."

"So what's that cough then?"

"Nothing to concern yourself with." Granny made a motion with her arm as if Bura were one of the annoying flies bothering Bela below.

Bura sat on the small three-legged stool, grasping the coarse red wool in her hands. "It is my concern, Grandmother." She hoped the full title would convey the sincerity she wanted to express. "What would I do without you?" she said, instead of what was really in her heart. *I'm not ready to lose you.* But it wasn't something Granny would be willing to hear, so it was easier to just pack it all in with the rest of her own shortcomings.

"Maybe you would finally marry. Not to one of these bastards, of course. But into the other village. I heard it's not that bad in Doshen Plana."

"Oh, yeah, of course. Or, maybe, I would just go down the mountain and find some rich merchant in Bag." Now it was Bura's turn to be affronted. Granny sounded serious, but she couldn't really be.

"Not everyone knows what your—"

"You know what, I don't care," Bura interrupted Granny before the woman could finish her thought. This wasn't a topic she wanted to entertain. "I don't mind being alone. So I don't care who knows or doesn't know what."

"I would die with less worry, knowing you're taken care of."

Bura furiously gripped at the blanket, but kept her mouth shut. She could've easily said how Granny had nothing but false hope. There was no man, no family, that would welcome her, not in Tzrni Dabar, not in Doshen Plana, not in any of the villages in between. It was a dream to think otherwise, but she couldn't begrudge Granny for wanting anything but safety for her. Maybe there would be a chance for a new life if she truly did go down the mountain, settle in Bag or on some of the islands—Pag or Rab, where the men from their village sold the wood for fuel or oars—but just the thought of going away made her throat clench and unsettled her, making her feel strange in her own skin. This was her home. The tall trees bending on a strong wind, the rustling a song well-known in her blood. The stiff cliffs towering over her head, breaking the clear skies, were her bones—her teeth, knuckles, and joints. She couldn't leave and replace this with the sea or busy towns. It would be easier to take off her own skin and let it hang on the wall, alongside her late grandpa's red cap.

"I just want you to take better care of yourself," Bura said in the end, again not saying what she truly wanted. The truth was that she was amazed at how the old woman didn't break under the tragedies the world stacked upon her shoulders. She'd been unbreakable when her daughter gave birth out of wedlock, while everyone was getting rocks in their hands, ready to throw the first one. She'd stood tall and proud when the war came and swept her husband and sons in its jaws, crushing them to nothingness, without even a grave they could visit. An unmoving stone, when life finally took away her only daughter, when she was left with nothing but one granddaughter, unwanted by anyone, even death. So many children died in Tzrni Dabar, taken by sickness and the hard life, yet Bura remained.

"You don't need to worry about me," Bura said. "You should worry about yourself. You're not getting any younger. Neither of us is."

But only one of them had trouble breathing and a heavy cough in her chest. When winter comes and snow falls, there would be no passages to the other villages, no way to Bag, to a doctor or medication. Why was Granny being so stubborn over this? Was she so tired of life that she wanted to die?

A cold feeling unrelated to the weather outside embraced Bura in a flash. Not even the wool in her hands could warm her up, nor the fire in the open hearth.

Granny wasn't done, though, because she slowly stood up, proud and sinewy, a fir so deeply rooted that no wind could ever break it. "I know how you feel. So, if you truly decide to stay on this solitary path," she continued, her voice deep, eyes full of a dangerous foreboding, "then you need to learn not to show weakness. Never show it in this place, which takes and it takes and it takes, always hungry for new blood." The words, similar to what Aunt Ika had said, made Bura feel uneasy since she had not expected to hear something like that from her own Granny. But it was easy to see the world as some horrible, gaping mouth, swallowing people up, when your own family had wilted away in a short amount of time before your eyes. Bura knew that feeling. The two of them were the last of their house. "Don't show it before me, nor before others, and especially not in front of the forest and the mountain. Do you understand?" She did, even when she wanted her Granny wasn't that stubborn over one woolen blanket. "Alright," Granny said. *"I'll pray to God to watch over you."*

With that, she gave Bura the wood carving she'd made over the fire. A little figurine of a wolf glistened in the orange light, its jaw open wide in a snarl.

That night, Bura dreamt her recurring dream. It always started the same, with a wind so strong the house shuddered from its attack. The wood creaked under the gusts, piercing her eardrums while her barley straw bed shook so hard it almost dissolved on the floor. She couldn't see Granny anywhere in the pitch darkness, but could still hear Bela's frightened mooing. Carefully, going on pure memory and instinct, she'd crawl towards the cellar.

There, illuminated by a strange greenish light, she could see the cow's beady eyes, so enlarged they almost popped out of her head, and a long black snake's body hooked on the udder with its fangs, suckling the cow dry. White fluid, mixed with scarlet drops, would dribble down the length of the snake's body, dropping slowly on its wrapped-up tail under the cow. Bura would've looked for an ax or a pitchfork to cut the snake in half, but her legs always turned to rock, becoming one with the mountain.

Sometimes, she was able to break free before waking up. Sometimes, she would scream and the wind would tear the house out from its foundation, a whirlwind taking away both the cow and the snake. This time, something was different. This time, the snake flexed its mouth, making it so large it swallowed the whole udder, while Bura was stuck in her place, and at that moment she finally woke up to the screeching of wood under the blows of the northern wind, getting ready for a storm.

In the morning, the storm still raged outside. It didn't rain, thankfully, but the wind picked up and didn't stop in its crusade. The branches of the nearby firs banged over their roof and windows as if trying to blast the house away from its place. It sounded like the wind was pleading, but she wasn't certain what for.

The rock-hard bread full of chaff grated under her teeth, making her gums ache while she chewed, falling on her hungry stomach like a stone. Milk didn't help, every taste of it reminded her of the dream, upsetting her insides even more. She tried to keep down her nausea long enough to eat her breakfast in peace, but it ended with her barely touching any food, which made it all even worse. In the meantime, she also had to act like everything was alright, like Granny wasn't coughing out liquid from her lungs, like they had all the food stock ready for the wintertime. It made her so angry—the bone-deep helplessness, knowing she couldn't do anything—that her blood soared in tandem with the wind outside.

Later, while Bura was in the middle of mending socks, Granny's coughing got so bad she almost fell into the boiling greens in the cauldron over the hearth. Bura jumped, discarded socks falling on the floor, forgotten.

"Granny!" she yelled, uselessly. She caught the old woman under her arms and helped her to the small straw cot. Upon touch, Bura could feel Granny burning up inside.

"I'm al—" Granny tried to say, but a shudder went through her instead, cutting off her words.

"You aren't alright, stop saying that!" Bura said, outyelling the wind's howl. Granny tried to fight her away, but she was too weak, too sick, so her granddaughter managed to force her into the bed. "Please, stop," she begged, and either it was something in her voice, or the tiredness Granny must've felt, because the old woman listened to her, for once. She let herself be tucked in under the wool, while Bura went to heat up the milk.

They had a little bit of honey, for emergencies, and Bura figured this was as good a time as any to use it, so she put two spoons of the golden nectar in the warming-up milk, for the cough.

"What did I say about showing weakness?" Granny

mused from her cot, suddenly a frail woman, wrinkled skin stretched thin over her skull, brown eyes sunken. Just yesterday, for Bura, she was everlasting like an evergreen tree. Now, she was nothing more than a branch, broken in half after the northern wind. "This will be the end of me."

"Don't be foolish, it's the fever talking," Bura answered, focusing on a simple task—getting the milk into Granny's cup so it doesn't drop all over the floor. Just so she didn't have to think about the possibility of losing the last of her family. The one who had been there for her all along.

"I've already lived a long life," Granny continued, "outlived my sisters, my mother, my husband, my children. Fifty years is a long time. Maybe it's time to admit that."

"You told me I had nothing to worry about, so what's with this talk of defeat?"

"And you told me I needed to stop saying everything was alright. You can't have it both ways."

Bura blinked the tears away from her eyes, taking a deep breath and closing the storm inside her. With a calm hand and a still face, she brought the cup to the bed, helping Granny sip on the warm, honeyed milk.

"What did you expect from a foolish girl? You know I'm never right," she tried to lighten the mood with a joke, but it fell flat.

With winter so close at their doorsteps, she couldn't wait much longer. No matter what Granny said, Bura wasn't ready to lose her yet. Prayers didn't do a thing, or their cow would already be immortal and Bura's mother would still be with them. But there must've been something she could do.

She sat by the hearth, watching the flames leap up

in dance, in her head going over a list of everyone she knew. The road to Bag was steep and treacherous but, mostly, it was a long way to go on foot. And there was no path through the valley for automobiles to reach them. There had to be someone who could help them, or let her borrow a horse. Only, she didn't know of anyone who would do that for her; risk helping her as if she were a leper who could pass her state to others just by associating with them. That meant no one from Tzrni Dabar, definitely. Just the thought of going from house to house to be turned away made her insides churn.

An idea slowly formed in her mind. The image of a face of the only person who had never seen her as anything other than a child, with kind words to soothe her wounds when the other children were too cruel. The memory of her young teacher helping her plant a seedling at the back of the school, just like the old teacher had done, many years ago. The pines still stood, strapping, in front of the building, shielding the school from strong winds, but Bura's small fir sapling had gotten trampled under the sheep.

Forming a plan, she stood up and started packing a small bundle—she would not take much, just one lanter, a half of a loaf, some cheese and milk, just in case, to keep her strength on the trek, or if she had to stay the night in the school, which was more than possible, given the time of day. The bigger problem was that they didn't have a lot of money she might use for the doctor, but there was some, hidden in an old jar, that she fished out.

"What are you doing?"

"Going to get some help."

"You can't be serious. What do you plan to do? Walk down the mountain?" Granny asked. "You know there is no one better with herbs than me around here, so who else would you try to get?"

"I know, but I can't leave you to your herbs and my honeyed milk. You need a doctor. City folk doctor. And, before you say another thing, I'm not walking. Remember my teacher? She will surely help me out. She has connections and a caring heart."

"A foolish girl, that's what you are. It's already midday outside. Evening will fall faster than you could reach the school. You can't go now. At least wait until tomorrow and go at dawn."

There was truth in Granny's words. She was still holding on, surely she won't die in the course of one day. If the dark catches Bura in the middle of the forest, how will she find her way to Ravni Dabar? How will she stay on the path and not fall and break her leg, or end her life as dinner in some beast's belly? How will she be of any help then? Just like Granny was the last one left of her family to take care of Bura, so was Bura for Granny, too.

A cough shook the old woman in the cot as if the disease itself was mocking her insecurity.

"I'm sorry. I need to do this now."

"Bura, Bura, please," Granny pleaded with her now, through coughing and tears. "Remember your cousin Ivica. Everyone else forgot, except for his poor mother. The forest took him; please don't rush into its open arms."

A tingle of a memory passed through Bura's mind, like a song she knew by heart, but couldn't recall its words anymore. A child's laughter, a punch, a scratched knee and a loose baby tooth. And a beheaded wolf, grinning from a pike. But it wasn't what Granny was supposed to say.

"Don't you mean *remember your mother*? Or have you forgotten your own daughter?" Bura knew she was being unnecessarily cruel to the old woman, especially when she saw how Granny's face fell upon hearing her words. If Granny refused to mention her daughter's disappearance in the forest, it was out of pain, not malice. An unwillingness to show weaknesses, Bura supposed. Not wanting the grief to consume her as it had Aunt Ika, Granny had once said. The erasure still hurt Bura, in a way Granny couldn't understand. "If you can get out of that bed without my help and get between me and the doors, then I'll stay and wait for tomorrow."

Granny watched her with huge muddled eyes, gritting her teeth so hard Bura could see the determination from her spot at the hearth. The old woman rapidly discarded the blanket from her body and lowered her legs on the floor. She gripped at the wooden leg of her cot, but when she started raising herself up, the coughing started up again, forcing her to bend down. She had to sit down, embracing her chest with her arms, like she was trying to stop her body from shattering apart.

Bura nodded. "Yesterday you could stand, today you're falling down. I'm not waiting for tomorrow." *You're the only one I have left in the whole wide world.*

Buckling down in the warmest clothes she could find, under Granny's watchful eyes, she lowered the crimson, knitted woolen hat over her ears and shawl of the same color over her neck and took a deep breath. Granny didn't have anything else to say, nor did she weep or beg. Bura didn't expect anything less. She still hoped this frown wasn't their last goodbye, before she took a step outside.

There was a gathering in the distance, in the village's center. The people there, some strangers, some not, were shouting and gesturing towards the forest. Aunt Ika, who stood at the back, caught Bura's curious gaze, her face a mask of vengeance. She nudged at the woodsman called Nuncle, pointing at Bura with her other arm. Not wanting to stay there a minute more to learn what all the fuss was about, especially not with the way Ika and Nuncle were watching her, like a lamb that needed to be ready for Eastern lunch, Bura turned and slipped between the firs, which would block her from sight.

Where a blowing wind soon caught her going against its current, a wall which tried—and failed—to stop her from getting into the depths of the black forest waiting behind her house.

Through the grayness and the mists of autumn, the colors and rains of spring, the brightness of summer and, sometimes, even the winter frost and snow—while it was still only a thin white cover on the ground—she had walked this path to the school. It wasn't easy, but it was usually doable. Now, though, it felt like the whole world was conspiring against her, to stop her from reaching her destination. She didn't even know the northern wind could blow in this direction.

Her steps met the rough ground with the uncertainty of a baby lamb. The forest creaked with unstoppable lamentations, branches bowing under a force more powerful than their trunks. For every two steps she made, the wind pushed her back one. Densely gathered clouds hid the sun, turning the world into dark grays and browns. The air carried a promise of snow. She was crawling at a slow pace, fearing that Granny had been right—that she wouldn't be able to reach the other village, Ravni Dabar, before night caught up with her. That all of this would end up being for nothing once the sun, already dimmed, fell behind the mountain's stone crown. Even if the night were clear, moonlight alone wouldn't be enough to light her way, not with the close-knit treetops, covering the skies.

Bura took a moment to compose herself, letting her fear fly away. This was her home, she knew every tree, every stone. If she turned back now, she would have to admit defeat and spend the night listening to her Granny slowly melting away.

With a silent rage, she braved the wind. She continued walking over treacherous grounds, the roots and small hills, holding herself upright by grabbing thin trunks and pushing herself away from them when she could. The northern wind was at her side the whole time, like a jealous lover keeping her in an ironclad embrace of its arms. The woods around her crackled and groaned, like a wounded beast's deep breathing.

The small amount of light dimmed further, turning the trees into moving shadows, and the ground into a gaping hole of a giant's wide-open mouth, ready to swallow Bura as soon as she stumbled and broke her bones and neck on the rocky path. She couldn't light her barn lantern yet, fearing she'll use up the kerosene before reaching her destination. She tried singing a song her mother had taught her once, when they were tending to the sheep—a long time ago, when they still had those—to distract herself from the high-pitched sounds.

A loud crack, like a shotgun blast, burst through the wailing wind. Bura wildly turned around and her eyes fell on a silhouette in the distance, half obscured by firs. It decidedly had shoulders and a head, as well as arms which were holding something long, with a fiery red eye. Its movement and build reminded her of Nuncle, but it could've easily been anyone else from her village. Fear gripped her heart, making it jump hoops.

The shadow moved the object in its hands, pointing the smoking eye towards the spot where Bura was standing. Not keen on waiting for what would happen next, she turned around and started running, disregarding the roots protruding from the ground and the dense growth of the trees, the trunks closing in on her like a noose. The wind picked its force back up, barreling at her front, like it was trying to get her to fly.

A burst of an earth-shattering sound reverberated in her ears. She staggered and lost her footing, falling down on the ground; hitting her head on a moss covered rock, her sight blackening.

For an immeasurable moment in time, everything was just cotton black. Then it unfurled into the smell of firs, grass and moss, the feeling of soil under her palms. The crawling of a bug over her face, its antennae touching her earlobe. With that came the panic, followed by a strike of her hand at the curious bug. The knowledge of where and why came last, and Bura frantically opened her eyes.

To a light, bluish gray tint of an early morning, clearing the haze in front of her. Trees, high above, the treetops green, unmoving and broad. The moss growing over the trunks. The silent woods, only a hint of a creak here, or a rustle there. The shadow of a man with a shotgun was nowhere in sight.

Bura's head hurt piercingly; touching her scalp made it burn. Her hand came back with a red splotch marring her fingers, already numb from cold. She watched the blood with the feeling of a stranger, a spectator to someone else's life, not like it were her own. Curiously empty of any thought. Like the wind had taken away her mind, leaving her just a shell on the ground.

It was only after recalling she'd had a hat which was now lost, that she finally woke up from her stupor. Anger simmered low in her gut, giving her strength to stand up even with her head still pulsing with a skull-tearing pain. A scream tried to get out of her mouth, already shaped in her throat, fighting to be let out into the wild. She tampered it down, having enough sense not to bring attention to herself, in case her attacker was still nearby.

Painstakingly slow, making sure she didn't make any loud movement, she checked her belongings. Everything was still there—the meager food, the shawl, the lamp still, thankfully, in one piece. Which couldn't exactly be said of Bura herself. There was an open wound on her temple, but it looked like, at least, it wasn't bleeding anymore. The scrapes and bruises covered her arms and palms where she fell on the ground, hands first. She couldn't see her knees, but felt a throbbing pain. Probably more bruises, then.

Worst of it all, though, it appeared that she'd lost the whole night. Bile burned in her throat with unshed tears. It was only after she'd furiously wiped at her eyes and tried to find her path again that she learned another important thing. She couldn't recognize the area she was in.

There was a vague familiarity to the forest. The firs, the spruce trees. But she wasn't on the old, worn-out path she's walked hundreds of times and, no matter how much she tried to orient herself, it felt all wrong.

Bura's legs scrambled in haste, regardless of the hurt knees or her split-open head. Her heart beat in the rhythm of a frightened bell. She just had to find the path again, and it couldn't be that far away, she hadn't run for a long time... she repeated it to herself over and over again. Everywhere her gaze fell, it was the same ground, the same trees moving in closer, obscuring her view. As if the forest had grown twice its size during the night, a net in which she was now caught, struggling to escape to no avail. In the absence of yesterday's wind, she could now feel every movement, every crack deep under her skin, as loud as the gunshot which had chased her away.

After almost slipping and falling again, she stopped to catch her breath and slow down her rushing heart. Coarse bark tingled under her palm where she'd put her arm on a great, wide spruce trunk. Her legs may have stopped, but the world continued expanding and contracting around her, twirling like smoke.

What's happening? a thought came not a moment too soon, when the unmistakable crackling of a broken branch echoed all around her. She hastily straightened herself up, her eyes fighting against the dark brown and gray morning haze, looking for anything which might be able to stand out against the monotone landscape. The crackling continued, another branch lost under someone's foot.

It was in front of her, walking towards her, so she took a step back. The undergrowth shook slightly, hiding a moving mass. Carefully, she took another step further away, her gaze never leaving the brown lump which was now slowly emerging in fully-fledged form. The fur had a sort of a rusted-brown shading to it, making her think of crusted blood, but the eyes underneath were as black as coals grabbed from the pits of Hell. The bear slobbered with a thin streak of saliva hanging from its lower jaw, glistening even in the dark of dawn. Its head was worthy of a hunter's wall, she thought, and the meat could feed her whole village for a few days. If anyone were to manage to kill this bear.

Clutching her bag, Bura nervously took another step back. If she started running, it would be the end of her. The robust animal just had to take a few large steps more to be upon her and to break her neck with its mighty jaws. Involuntarily, her gaze fell on its paws, bigger than her fists, the claws so sharp they could probably make gaping wounds in the thick trunks around her.

The bear raised its head, sniffing the air, but its eyes never left hers. Those deep orbs, brimming with hunger and hate.

Standing on its hind legs, the bear let out a blood-chilling roar, shattering the silence between them. Without giving her a chance, it charged at her, a barreling bulk made of canines and claws. Bura didn't even have the time to move; she raised her arms on instinct, a futile move, when the strongest force brushed past her, almost throwing her down on the ground.

She hit her head again, her teeth knocking into each other so hard she tasted blood. Her gums hurt as if she'd tried to eat through a dozen stinging bees. But her eyes managed to stay open, and she didn't lose her senses like the last time she'd fallen. That's why she could now see two blurred masses clashing at each other, their wild snarling a thundering sound in the quiet. For a moment, she thought it was another bear fighting over the right to eat her first. After blinking the confusion away, her eyes focused on a slender body and a long muzzle, a tail so bushy and long it swept at the undergrowth during the fight.

She gulped, remembering the figurine Granny had carved. I'll pray to God to watch over you.

A wolf, the size of a bear, its fur as dark as night personified, was snapping at the bear's neck, biting out big chunks of meat, making blood sail through the air and spray the trunks, the moss and Bura, on the ground. With two woodland beasts fighting over her, she didn't plan on sticking around to see who would have the honor of eating her alive. She started scrambling away. Her sight darkened as soon as she stood up on two shaky legs, and she lost her footing again with the stinging pain. The woods twirled around her in a twisted dance of black spots and green shapes. She swallowed up the bile rising in her throat, before she could puke it out, the nasty, bitter taste lingering on her tongue.

For a brief, fleeting heartbeat everything was quiet

again while her vision swam. A moment of uttermost stillness washed over her, goosebumps rising on her neck. It was in that moment, when the world before her eyes stopped moving and her sight sharpened, that she felt, more than understood, what the silence behind her back meant.

She was still alive, at least. Maybe the animals have killed each other. Bura prayed that, when she turned around, both the wolf and the bear would be in shredded stripes, only good for a home-cooked meal. She would scoop up the meat that she could carry with her, and the bear's paws, of course, go back home and make venison stew.

But that would not heal Granny and, besides, prayers never worked for her. Which she was reminded of upon turning around and coming eye to eye with the reflecting gaze of the wolf, who had crept close to her in complete silence.

Bura grasped her shawl, fury igniting her blood. It wasn't fair. If she died here, she would be just another Granny's girl who'd gone into the woods, never to come back. Granny would finally stay all by her lonesome, the last of her family dying before her. Only to, probably, join them soon enough herself, because there was no one in the village to care enough to help her out. Or maybe, with Bura gone, things would change for Granny, but for the better.

"Granny was right, I am a foolish girl," she said to the wolf, like it could understand. It was probably because of that look of pure intent in the small, narrow eyes, the sign of intelligence she didn't expect. Crimson blood, sprinkled all over the dark fur, mixed the black with red. It wasn't snarling nor growling, just watching at her with a burning intensity. Angry gashes riddled its back in places where bear claws had managed to get a hold and rip at the skin and meat.

The bear, on the other hand, lay completely still, a mangled heap, the head almost completely bitten away from the body. This is what Bura would look like to someone else, torn apart, left in pieces, if she didn't figure out how to get away. How to fight.

The wolf jerked its head. It made a snorting sound, like some of the blood had gotten into its nostrils and now it couldn't breathe normally. A shudder passed through its body, from the tail to its head. And it didn't stop there.

Bura was too confused to move. Maybe she was lucky, she thought while the beast twitched, its throat making a half-choking, half-puking sound, and the wolf was fatally wounded indeed, just stubborn enough to stay alive for a few minutes longer. But then its front legs broke before her eyes, white sharp bone protruding towards her, bathed in blood. Bura gasped, completely locked in place. The wolf looked at her with those strange, smart eyes, full of light, when its head twisted on the neck, making a splitting sound. The skin fell apart, just slipped from the skull. Furry ears dangled over the ground, the skin under the skull hanging by a loose thread still connecting it to the neck.

It didn't stop there, either. Bura watched with horrified interest as the bones cracked open under unseen blows—dozens of straight lines forming in the skull, breaking it apart; legs, ribs and spine rupturing, splintering, debris falling away in chalky dust. The meat and organs fell to the ground with a thumping sound. Under all that gore, a new head emerged from the blood, then shoulders, then the rest of the body—slender arms, breasts, stomach and strong legs—until Bura's eyes finally accepted what they were seeing.

Covered in bloody remains of a wolf, a beautiful woman stood, as naked as a newborn child. Her dark hair was slicked with crimson liquid, both on her head and in other places Bura definitely shouldn't have seen, but couldn't really help herself. Her eyes wandered, drinking it all in, trying to understand. She gaped with her mouth wide-open.

"I—" she started, then stopped. Her mind completely blank. And her gaze still had a hard time fixing at one place. Like, for example, at the woman's face and her golden-brown eyes.

"Fear not. I'm not here to hurt you," the woman said. Her voice was something else. Bura could feel it like a fire burning hotly in their open hearth at home, while the winter storms raged outside, or smell it like freshly baked barley bread. None of those were sounds, and yet, her mind remembered them upon hearing the woman talk.

"What are you?" Bura asked, coming back to something resembling her common sense. Her mind was still disagreeing with her eyes.

The woman smiled through blood on her lips, a crooked smile, before collecting the wolf's pelt from the ground. The one she'd shed like a snake. "Actually, the question should be *where*, not what."

Bura blinked in confusion while the woman wrinkled her nose, looking around as if she were seeing the forest for the first time. "Where? Are you from?"

The woman shrugged. The movement attracted attention to her chest and Bura quickly jerked her eyes back to the woman's face, feeling her cheeks burn.

It wasn't her fault the woman was standing there stark naked.

"Not from here, I'll tell you that," the woman finally answered, returning her gaze to Bura, who was still half-laying, half-leaning on the ground. "From far away," she added, jerking her head upwards.

Did she mean from the mountain tops? They weren't that very far.

The woman covered herself with the wolf pelt, the front paws hanging at her chest, the wolf head almost a hood on her hair. The gaping hole where the teeth should go hung loosely over the woman's face.

"We should try and find a way to get out of this place."

"Well, yeah..." Bura mumbled through her burning cheeks, "that's what I was trying to do when the bear... when you..." She still couldn't understand how this was possible; she must've lost her mind with the blow. Maybe she had died, and this was some sort of limbo, where wolves turned into beautiful women to... do what, exactly? Guide Bura to her own circle of Hell? It wouldn't be that bad, if that were the case.

The wolf woman reached out her hand towards Bura, who was still spread out under her, puzzled. The palm was sticky with blood, but Bura accepted it with her own hand. The grip was strong and the woman pulled her up. Bura feared that she would black out again, and then thought that, maybe, it wouldn't be that bad if it meant that this stranger would catch her in her arms. Warmth radiated from the woman's form, and Bura wanted to touch it, leaning closer than propriety allowed, but who cared? She was bruised, lost in the middle of the woods, had been shot at and almost gotten mauled by the bear. She deserved this one thing.

"Thank you," Bura said, remembering that this woman had saved her life, no matter how impossible all of this was. Like something out of one of Granny's tales. Wasn't there a story about shapeshifters in which, if someone stole their pelt, they had to stay human and marry that person? Something like that.

A memory of her mother claiming that Bura's father had been a wind resurfaced in that moment, and she had to stifle a maniacal burst of giggling. Who knows; if there are people able to change their shape, maybe the wind really could father a child.

"Oh, no need for thanks," the woman replayed, grinning with white teeth which looked mighty sharp. Her gums looked healthy and pink too, Bura noticed, entirely aware of the throbbing pain and metallic taste in her own mouth.

"I'm Bura." She was still holding the woman's hand, standing so close she could feel her breath on her own face. At least it was easier to keep her gaze on her face like this.

"Like the northern wind?" the woman asked, her eyebrows rising in an almost perfect arc.

"Long story," she said, not really in the mood to explain how she got the name.

"Dorja."

Bura heard the word, but didn't really understand what it meant, too focused on looking at the woman's full lips. And then it hit her. It was the woman's name, very pointedly not from these parts, for she'd never heard it before. So she really was from somewhere far away. "Thank you again, Dorja."

"Save your thanks for when you're out of this forest."

The way it was spoken chilled Bura to her bones, making it obvious Dorja didn't expect to be able to do it easily. Which was curious—after all, she was a wolf who'd just fought off a giant bear. But her eyes were serious, concerned, dropping the light banter from before.

"I know I'm lost, but I don't think that I'm that far away from my home. My village should be close," Bura tried to explain, fighting against a rising dread. First, she should focus on getting out. Then she can worry about Granny again.

Dorja looked at her as if she were a child who was still struggling with letters. Bura didn't like it, all. She finally let go of the woman's arms and took a step back, clearing her head. Just because the woman was a wolf, beyond beautiful, and had saved her life, didn't mean Bura should lose her mind in clouds.

"You're thinking with your head," Dorja said, her eyes sad, but hard, like Bura's leftover bread. "Ignore that noise, and try doing it with your heart." And to demonstrate the point, she put her warm hand on Bura's chest.

The touch was soft and light, in stark contrast with how strong her grip was. It shattered Bura's thoughts into miniscule pieces, easily scattered in the wind. In that emptiness of mind, one thought managed to stick. *How the hell should I think with my heart?*

Bura watched Dorja's eyes closely, looking for her answers there. They were like sunlight caught in a jar, making Bura a moth who happily flew to her doom. She shook her head, letting go of confusing thoughts, turning towards the trees instead. Looking closely at the branches, she tried to ignore what was on the surface of it all. Letting her mind wander, focusing more on the way things felt, than the shapes they had.

She could feel the sharpened teeth in a jaw, waiting, open, before closing on unsuspecting prey. Hunger, bigger than her stomach, opening up like a hole vaster than the sky. Darkness falling upon the woods, hiding men with blades, with guns, fighting over sheep and cows, before dropping dead and feeding the mountain with their blood. The constant need, burrowing under her skin, to kill, to maim, to consume.

The trees didn't look like firs and spruces anymore. They were a growth which couldn't be stopped, which ruled over the world.

It wasn't her forest anymore; instead, it was very much blocking the way for her to get home again. Keeping her in place.

"I don't understand," she said, so quietly she wasn't certain Dorja could hear her.

"This place doesn't know time. Or, at least, it knows only of before. But we shouldn't be still. Come." Dorja took her hand again, and Bura let her do that. "Let's walk."

Bura, feeling like she was watched from behind, didn't have anything to object to that.

It didn't get lighter with the passing of time, that same haziness of early morning clinging to the air instead, making it hard to see farther in the shadow of the woods. The sun should've been high in the sky long ago, the rays bursting through the green needles of the treetops. Instead, Bura felt like walking through ash.

"I don't understand how I could've come to these strange woods. I took a path I know well." This wasn't just some previously undiscovered part of her forest, she understood it now. What she didn't understand was how she could've stumbled into unfamiliar territory, like it was simply a new shepherd's cabin she'd found hidden in the hill.

"It's hard to explain. You didn't stray from the path so much as... well, walk through the door, usually locked, but suddenly open wide up."

"What?"

"Like I said, it's hard to explain."

"How did you get here?" Bura voiced her wonder, a thousand questions swimming in her head. "Or are you going to say it's also hard to explain?"

Dorja looked at her from under the hollow pelt obscuring half her face. Her eyes burned in the shadow of the fur, and white teeth glistened in the dark. "Exactly that." There was a joking tone in her voice.

Bura frowned and bit her lip, but kept following the other woman, with no other course for her to take. She didn't want to stay alone in the middle of the trees which wanted to swallow her.

Walking helped her limbs stay warm, but her cheeks still felt the biting of the cold. Her long, light hair was tangled, crusted in blood, weighing her down, but it didn't do much to keep the chillines at bay, so she mourned the loss of her hat. Dorja, on the other hand, was completely naked under the fur, but didn't shiver, her teeth didn't chatter, and her steps were sure. She didn't look like she was freezing her ass off.

"Aren't you cold?" Bura couldn't help but ask.

Maybe there was more to magic than just changing one's shape. She wondered how that worked, but it only made her head hurt more.

"No. I have thicker skin than that." And again, that crooked smile. It was grating on her nerves, and Bura really wanted to swipe it off Dorja's face.

With every passing step, the undergrowth densed, grabbing at her legs with its torny hands. Bura knew there was something else she needed to do, and soon, but the thought of it made her heart beat like a hammer. Not here, in these wicked woods.

The wind picked up a bit, rustling in the leaves.

"Ah, Dorja?"

"Hm?" The woman didn't even stop, starting down a rocky slope.

"I need to pee," Bura confessed, sparks lighting up her face, as soon as Dorja turned and pierced her with a pointed look.

"So pee. I'll wait."

Bura rolled her eyes. Peeing wasn't the problem. The forest was. But she knew it wasn't something she could just skip doing. Sighing, she took cover behind a tall bush and raised her skirt, doing something she did all the time in her life. Yet the dream of the snake sucking on the udder flashed before her eyes in the worst moment. There weren't any snakes around, it was too cold for them; she tried to reason with her mind. But her insides were still clenched, and her mind's eye conjurened an image so vivid; a predator slightly slithering, preparing its fangs.

She got up so fast she almost blacked out again. Her heart beat faster, in sync with the rhythm of the wind whispering in the high branches.

It's come back, she noted for the first time. The

morning—or, at least, that moment when she opened her eyes—was calm, but now it appeared it would be another windy day.

"Everything alright?" Dorja asked her, a few steps away, her face partially turned to the side. She was nursing a frown, but Bura didn't know what about.

"Yes, I just don't like this place." It hated her, that much was obvious. The trees didn't have eyes, but their trunks were claws and teeth, as sharp and menacing as a bear's.

"Nor should you." Dorja's pelt was fluttering around her, and she watched it with a deepening frown. "I didn't expect the wind. I don't like this. We should move faster."

"Do you even know where we're going? It feels like walking in circles." Everything was the same—the colors blurring together, making it hard to orient herself.

They walked up a hill, then down a slope; passed rows upon rows of dark trunks, their rich treetops almost closing the view of the skies. She couldn't even guess which of the cliffs they were walking towards. But Dorja didn't look lost, in fact, she walked with confidence. Bura tried to stop her suspicions from showing in her face.

"I have a good idea, so yes. Well, no." Dorja frowned. "I mean, I've never been here before, but even if it weren't for that, this forest would do everything in its power to keep us here. But I'm not the ordinary wolf, either. I can sense which way is the true one." She turned to face Bura fully. "And I guess you could, too, if you knew how."

A strange emotion passed through Bura at the thought, fear mingled with apprehension, frustration and a general dislike. A memory dredged up again, her mother's warm face while she was telling Bura about her father under pale blue skies. Bura had been wide eyed and full of wonder at that time; now old enough not to believe in stories. At least, she thought it was just a lie her mother had transformed into a fairy tale; a wind sweeping her mother away and leaving behind a seed that turned into Bura. But now, looking at Dorja, she was starting to doubt her conviction. Maybe her mother had simply skipped the part where the wind turned into a handsome man. What did that mean for her, though?

"Well, I'm a very ordinary human, so I don't see why I should be able to do that," Bura said, hiding her inner turmoil.

"Hm." Dorja looked like she wanted to say something, when a loud, grumbling sound interrupted them.

Bura's face burned in shame, while the other woman's eyes dropped to her belly.

"Do you have any food?" Dorja asked.

"Some cheese, a little bit of milk and half a loaf of bread." Even if the latter would probably be better used as a weapon.

"Damn, we should've taken some bear with us." Dorja sighed, her lovely face scrunched in disappointment. "Alright, no matter. I hope we'll get out soon and, if we don't, I'll catch some food for you. Come now, we should take a break and this is not the best place." She motioned at the slope they were standing on, an easy place to lose their footing and fall on.

It would be the worst nightmare if she learned that this was all some sort of a twisted game for the wolf-woman's amusement. Keeping Bura safe, giving her comfort, only to eat her later. Granny told her that meat tasted better if the sheep didn't know they were getting ready for slaughter. Bura bit her lip, shivering, this time for a different reason altogether.

She still held onto Dorja as they descended, because she was a pathetic sucker, starved for touch.

"Here, sit here." Dorja showed a huge rock sticking from the ground.

"Do you want some?" She offered her rations to Dorja, with a bitter hope that the woman would refuse. There wasn't enough for both of them, and Bura was half-dead on her feet even without adding hunger to the mix.

"No, it's alright, I already ate." Bura had to carefully close her expression, trying to hide her relief, but she must've done a poor job because Dorja smiled a sad, pitying smile which spoiled the taste of the cheese in Bura's mouth.

She ate through resentment, watering it down with milk. The small amount of food made her only crave for more. It was getting colder, and sitting only helped the wind to seep under her clothes, freezing her skin and bones. Bura embraced herself, feeling her teeth start to clutter. The air before her mouth turned white.

"How much more, what do you think?" she asked Dorja, who had been looking at her the whole time, standing above Bura, leaning at an almost black fir tree pulsing in front of Bura's eyes. Dorja's wolf pelt danced in the air, flapping on the wind, but she still managed to keep it on her body.

"It depends."

"On what?"

"How hungry its master is."

The chill in Bura's heart had nothing to do with the cold air. "Master?" A deep, open mouth, sucking in the blood, the life. The yellow eyes, a lantern in the night, luring the lost souls into the waiting hole.

"There is no land that doesn't belong to someone. Just because there's no human to claim it doesn't mean there are no masters taking care of it. Sometimes, even when humans do try to take a piece for themselves, it doesn't mean the original master will go away." Dorja's eyes were two deep pits, tempting Bura to fall into them. Her voice dripped with knowledge beyond Bura's comprehension. "What do you know of your history?"

The question caught her off guard. Did she mean her own, or the village one? She played it safe. "I know Dilinoga was the first to build himself a home in these lands. He had to cut down and burn through the rainforest to make pasture for his cattle. And when he built his home, his family came, and with them, the others," Bura recited. His descendants in the village were still mighty proud of their ancestor. The first one to tame the valleys this deep in the mountain range.

"And before him?"

Bura shrugged. "People were using this land for cattle but no one really lived here? I think?" She thought harder. "There were Turks here at some point." The only reason she knew of it was because Dilinoga's family still boasted how he stole Turkish cattle and even killed some Turkish foes. Which were, well, pretty much any Turks passing over the mountain. But that was so long ago, and new wars had come and swept through the land, new enemies for the people of the valleys popping up like mushrooms after the rain. She shook away her morose thoughts, focusing on the present. "Why are you asking me this?"

"Because people once knew there were places one shouldn't mess around with. Or, if they did do it, that proper gifts should be given in return, at least. Your people forgot that. These woods did not. That's why this place, and your home, exist on a very slippery slope."

Bura shivered in the wind. "What does that mean?" She didn't like the way the other woman was constantly talking in riddles. It made her feel like a child again, listening to her teacher's lessons.

"It means that the Illyrians, who walked these hills once upon a time, always made sacrifices to the land. Even the Turks and your Dilinoga knew that blood needs to be spilled once in a while to keep the peace. In this new day and age, you people have forgotten that. But the gods did not." Bura's eyebrows arched so high, she felt her own face probably made for a ridiculous sight. Dorja noticed her incredulous look, so she continued with her tale: "Yes, *gods*. This whole mountain was the home of a god once." She put up a clawlike finger, like she suddenly remembered something. "Or maybe the *mountain* is a *god*. It's sometimes not clear with things this ancient."

Bura suddenly remembered Aunt Ika's mumbling nonsense at the village well, about the hungry land and her lost son, just the day before yesterday. Her insistence that they should give up Bura before losing another innocent child.

Before going into the woods, she'd seen Ika with Nuncle, telling him something. Was he the one who had shot at Bura, wishing to make a sacrifice? Is that why she was here, in this twisted version of her own forest?

A land outside of time, Dorja had told her. Did she mean the time before they'd destroyed the mountain's rainforest, reshaping it to a liveable place?

"How do you know all this?" she asked, a suspicion still gnawing at her feet. She knew that the villagers wanted her gone—she was a stain on their honest, hard-working life. A bastard with an unknown father, unwed herself, in a village proudly boasting of having no separations, spinsters or bachelors. Dorja, on the other hand, was a stranger, her motives hidden under a double set of skins. No matter how beautiful Dorja was, how tempting her voice, or just because there was no other way for Bura to survive, she couldn't just blindly follow her around.

"I was taught about this place," Dorja said after a longer silence which didn't really give a lot of credence to her sentence.

"Taught? By whom? And why?" Bura was relentless. Her life depended upon it.

The pelt hung over Dorja's face, hiding most of it under the wolf's skin. But she could still see the woman's chin, pursed lips, and one intense eye.

"My own god," Dorja said in a quiet voice, almost a whisper. She flinched at the last word, looking over her shoulder as if checking if the trees had heard her. "But we shouldn't mention them here. The two of them... mine, and this one, they used to fight over this mountain. Until an understanding was made. My... patron can do what they want out there, in your world, but they can't get over here. So we don't want to attract more attention than we already have."

Bura wanted to ask more, her mind full of stormy thoughts. The wind was blowing over their heads, playing with branches.

If there were gods, why weren't her prayers working?

Maybe she'd just been praying to the wrong one all this time. Maybe she should've just taken Bela into the woods and slit her throat.

"Is this something you do regularly? Find lost girls and then confuse them even more?" Bura joked, but there was a biting undertone to her words.

The other woman laughed and the sound rang sweetly. "No, this is definitely a first. My tasks are more along the side of keeping the various woodlands my patron rules over in check, than keeping company to beautiful women." Hearing that, Bura blushed. "I'm sorry. Look." Dorja sighed and crouched in front of Bura, coming face to face with her. "I understand what this must feel like. Being completely out of your depth. It's not my wish to make things worse. Truly, I would like nothing more than to explain everything you wanted to know. To show you anything you wanted to see. But this is neither the time, nor the place."

No, Bura understood that. She should focus on getting back home, finding a new way to help Granny. Maybe, after that, she'd have the time to sit down with Dorja and listen to her tales. To learn about the wolf-woman and the world outside her own home.

Snowflakes, so miniscule, but bright white in the dim grayness of the world, started falling down. Twirling in front of Bura, sticking to her cheeks and mouth. Dorja opened a palm before her, catching some in her hand.

"Hm. This is... unexpected," Dorja said, watching Bura with a gaze so peculiar it made her feel like it was her own fault it had started to snow. The wind picked up, too, and Bura had to strain her ears to hear

Dorja over the howling. "Come, we're running out of time."

The snow didn't wait for too long before it started falling with intensity, huge white flakes dropping almost vertically under the strong gusts of wind. Bura's ears were freezing, uncovered in the air, so she took off her shawl and put it over her head and ears, binding it under her throat. She hid her hands in the pockets of her coat, even though a part of her still wanted to take Dorja's hand. Snow was getting in her eyes, making it hard to see. Everything was suddenly a bright whiteness she had to fight against, with her sight and shivering body.

"Please, please, please, please, please..." a child whispered in Bura's ears. Her legs stopped abruptly as she looked for the source of the sound. The voice was familiar in a way which itched her brain—it was just there, like a memory of a dream before it slipped away with the morning sun. It hurt her teeth, this unknowing, until she figured out that she'd been gritting them together and loosened her jaw.

Dorja's back continued down the path, gliding between the trees like they were not even there. Bura hurried after her, afraid to lose the wolf pelt from sight. In the hurry, her foot got caught on a root and she almost lost her balance. The root was bulging out from the ground, like a hand which had tried to catch her. When she raised her head, she came eye to eye with a huge spruce which, she was certain, wasn't there before. It was blocking out her view of Dorja.

Her heart almost jumped out of her chest, and she bypassed the tree, only to catch a glimpse of the black fur moving deeper into the woods amongst the trees which were now turning towards Bura, their branches fighting against the wind.

"Dorja!" she tried to yell, but her voice was lost, drowned in the moans of the forest.

Bura started towards where she'd last seen the wolf pelt, but the *please, please, please, please* caught up with her again. The voice was flying freely on the northern wind, along with the snowflakes; it was everywhere around her, covering her like a blanket, or her shawl. Mixing with the wailing, with her heartbeats, with the crackling of the branches. It tapped her brain lightly, and brief flashes passed in front of her eyes. Scraped knees. Children's laughter. The *bastard*, the *freak*, the *my dad says they should've left you in the forest for the wolves to eat.* Someone got in front of her, a fight broke out, blood dropped on the hungry ground. And Bura ran, ran, ran as fast as the wind, until she was at her school, in the safety of her teacher's arms.

Please, the wind begged. She took out her hands from the pockets, freeing the vulnerable skin to the freezing bites. There was something deep in her, now waking up, a slight touch of panic, but tangled with a strange calmness. Like she knew what she had to do; it was just that her brain was the last one to get to hear the plan. *Please*, said the child in her ear, the cool air blowing under her shawl.

Carefully closing down on her fear—which still begged her to run, to hide, to find Dorja; the self-preservation instinct which had given her the boost to run through the woods in record time—she extended her right arm behind her back. Palm up. A cold hand, made of snowflakes, took it. Snow fell on her skin, melting. But the strong grip was there, and it started pulling her away from where Dorja had gone to.

When she turned around to be able to walk face forward to where the child was taking her, there was no one to be seen. Just her arm, hanging in the air, completely empty. But she could still feel the touch, as surely as she was able to feel Dorja's while the other woman was holding her.

The snow was blowing at her back and the trees moved in their rooted spots to clear her path. The rocky ground under her feet shook, the roots disappearing under the surface, the undergrowth bowing so she could easily pass through. The whole forest changed so she could walk onward as if she were on a cloud.

Until everything cleared away and she found herself in front of a cave's opening. The darkness of the maw gorged on the wind, the snow stopping just short of it. The cold hand gripped her harder as she faltered for the first time in this short trek. There was no going back.

The mouth of the cave pulsed with warm air currents and a strange light as if the sun, caught in a web, illuminated the space. Inside, near the entrance, bodies littered the walls and the ground, dried-out shells which had once encapsulated meat, bones and organs. There was nothing there now. Something had eaten all of the insides, leaving the skin behind. There were clothes and weapons, too, old-looking axes, sabers and swords, but firearms, too—guns and shotguns, as well as uniforms, some she couldn't even recognize. Her eyes hurriedly wandered over the leftovers, a knot in her throat as she tried to remember what her mother had worn the day she went into the forest, never to return.

A small gasp managed to escape from her when she recognized the hat, buried under similar red ones. She walked over to it, careful not to step on anyone's remains, and took the article of clothing covered in dust and dirt.

"*Please*," Ivica said, and the bright, sunny day broke out in her head. She was walking behind the others, like always, afraid; following the bigger kids to school, clutching her bag at her chest. Ivica was the only one who smiled at her encouragingly, while no one else was looking, of course. It still helped her feel more at ease, while she was so alone, without her mother or Granny at her back to protect her. A mistake. To feel like that. The first time they'd gone to school nothing happened, the others just ignored her, like she wasn't even there. Nor did the second or the third time. But when it did, when the kids turned on her, mocking and cruel, and when Ivica jumped in to defend her, she ran away. Left him behind. And he never came back.

"Bura?" Dorja's voice found her while she was crying all over the small hat, a bag and a set of clothes she'd managed to untangle from the rest. "Bura!" the other woman growled—a shout that she needed to turn down into a whisper.

Strong arms caught Bura's shoulders, shaking her.

"What is wrong with you?" Dorja asked, fury lightening her eyes, turning them into fiery orbs like twin suns. "You just disappeared. I almost didn't manage to find you with the snowstorm covering your tracks and smell."

"I'm sorry." Bura knew how pathetic that sounded. She didn't have words to explain how she felt or what she did. The storm raging outside the cave could not compete with the one that howled inside of her.

"This is the last place we should be right now. Come!" The wolf-woman's arms were strong, but Bura did not budge. She was as hard as a rock built into the foundations of the mountain.

"You don't understand," Bura whispered, so she wouldn't disturb the dead. They were standing all around them, thin whispers of air, flames extinguished on the candle, only a flowing smoke left behind. "Ivica is here. He needs my help."

Dorja cursed under her breath. Her face, covered in crusted blood she still didn't have the time to wash out, was scrunched in thought. She was, also, not entirely happy. "Okay, I'll bite. Who's Ivica?"

Bura showed the clothes in her arms as if that should explain everything. "We were relatives, but not close. The other children, well, they weren't entirely kind to me. I'm a bastard. Everyone knew I didn't have a dad, and the grownups in the village had a lot to say about that. Once, the older kids tried to rough me up a bit, because, why not, their dads said it would be better for the village if I were dead. We were all in the middle of the forest, on the trek to school. So Ivica jumped to defend me. Got into a fight. And I run away." She finished her tale, but by the impatient look in Dorja's face, she figured she didn't tell the most important part. One that everyone in the village knew, but she made herself forget. "Ivica never came back. The other kids left him alone in the woods, and he never came home. The others said it was the wolves. But I guess he found his way into the same passage that brought me here."

Dorja's voice was full of razor-sharp sadness, one

that sounded like a cry on the full moon. "It's not your fault."

"I know. But he's stuck. He's pleading for help. I couldn't help him before. But I might be able to help him now."

Dorja was watching her with a new look, one Bura didn't really recognize. It wasn't the pity she'd seen before, nor sadness. It was something else entirely, and it carried an edge that stoked the fire in Bura's stomach.

"And you know how? Do you see where we're standing?" Dorja pointed out the scattered remains, the gulping path which led deeper into the cave.

"You said I could find my way. Only if I knew how. Help me do this thing." There were still questions over Dorja's involvement which Bura hadn't forgotten. Her sudden appearance. All the knowledge she had. The god she served. But this was not the time to voice them. Bura will just have to believe that the other woman was truly her ally, and not against her.

"You are so brave, do you know that?" Dorja's voice was quiet, but her eyes were nothing but.

Bura shook her head. "I'm just a girl who wants to right a wrong."

The wolf-woman looked at her in clear disbelief. "You don't even know what you are," she said, and Bura's curiosity flared. "But you'll have to find it in yourself soon, if you want us to survive. Alright, I hope I'm not making a mistake that'll end in your death," she said in the end, keeping her shedded skin tightly in her hands.

Bura stood up, glancing over the drained souls, only an echo of persons that they were before. The only body that was missing was her mother's. That would be too easy, too clean. A closure she so desperately wanted, to the point she was hoping her mother had fallen like a sacrifice to some old, forgotten god. Rather than just lost in the forest.

Ivica waited there, a solemn wall of condensed wind, snowflakes hanging arrested midair. She nodded towards him, a goodbye of sorts or, maybe, the thanks she didn't get to tell him earlier. With a deep breath, and a wolf standing on two legs behind her back, she faced the path towards the rest of the cave.

The farther they left the opening behind, the more that strange light stayed outside of their reach. Darkness swept in with each step. Dorja's eyes reflected in the dark, but Bura had trouble keeping her sight, so she took out her lantern and lit it up. The soft yellow light bloomed between the damp walls, shadows shifting away from where her hand moved to. With her lantern illuminating the way, Bura continued down the path, Dorja never straying too far away.

The walls constricted around them, closing in on them, the space becoming more cramped. A slight pulsing could be heard, reverberating from the solid rock that shook, ever so slightly, in front of their eyes. Like a throat gulping, swallowing down the food. The ground changed its texture, from stone to the wet, slimy body that was wrapping around itself. Like entangled rope, thick as a tree trunk. Or a snake, so big it could swallow down the whole mountain. Moisture dripped from the ceiling, cold drops falling on Bura's forehead and nose, reminding her of blood.

Dorja put her arms around Bura's shoulders, getting so close she could feel the warmth radiating from her body. The cave was tightening, the walls so close that, if she moved her arms, she could touch them now. Dorja's breath on her neck was comforting, giving her strength to continue down to what looked like the belly of the beast.

She had been worried about Dorja's motives, but was now willingly walking through the insides of a god with her, letting herself, and the other woman, be devoured.

When it looked like the darkness had gotten so condensed that not even Bura's lantern could get through it, a moan resounded from up ahead, calling to them. The small yellow light touched upon a hole in the wall—a portal, or a door, to a chamber.

Dorja squeezed her shoulder. There was no turning back. Hoping she didn't make a mistake, Bura led them through the doors into the living dark.

Her lantern's light became a small speck of yellow in the black oil that was so heavy Bura could barely breathe. She could scarcely see the outline of her hand which was holding the light, anything beyond an impossibility. Knowing it was futile to try and see with her eyes, she closed them, focusing on sounds.

The walls and the ground pumped, a deafening sound in the undisturbed quiet of the place. She had to pick her steps carefully, feeling the constant shifting under her feet. In the midst of it, there was her own breathing and Dorja's, close behind. And, beyond all of it, a slight moaning broke out, in pauses. Something dripped on Bura's head, burning her, leaving an acidic smell. A hiss of pain escaped her lips and she put a palm over her mouth to stop herself from making another sound.

A heavy burden suddenly covered her—the smell of blood overtaking every other sense. The wolf pelt; she knew as soon as something warm, squishy and suspiciously skinlike fell over her face, protecting it from the acid. Nodding her head in thanks as if the other woman could see her, Bura slowly crept over the rising and falling ground, towards the source of the painful, muffled cries.

The closer she came, the denser the air got; like walking through a toxic fog, with a rotten sulfur smell. Her heart beat a strong, drumming rhythm, her blood boiling to the point she didn't even feel cold anymore. She was a walking wind, finally blowing through the last gates which could've kept it at bay. Where she walked, a bura sang, and the walls groaned as if under attack. But she, herself, was untouched, her step steady and right. The cave broke out in full-blown shivers, felt in the air, sensed in the soles of her feet. She stood tall and unflinching, a rock in the middle of the river.

She walked, until she couldn't any more, coming to an obstacle, a wall. Knowing it was futile to even try to see in this essence of the dark, she dropped the lantern on the ground, leaving her arms to do the seeing.

Her fingers touched the wet stone, flat on the surface. She slowly inched over it, hearing the moaning from a closer proximity than ever before. Slinking her fingers towards it, she came to a protrusion in the stone, a lump quite big, slippery, almost rubberlike. It was pulsing under her fingers, thrumming with blood. She followed its shape, overlapping in and on itself, breaking through, disentangling it until she found a soft, chubby face beneath all of it.

Grasping the meaty, moaning head, probably belonging to a live child, she started ripping the body off the wall. Snakelike polyps hung onto it, fighting against her, burrowing in its body in many spots. She groaned in frustration, feeling Dorja at her side, helping her. They moved together, finally tearing out the moaning child from the gulping wall.

One of the polyps detached and fell on Bura's hand. A stabbing pain, like nothing she'd ever felt before, exploded in her arm. She felt her blood rushing towards the sucking mouth, and she let the long buried scream erupt from her mouth. The mountain itself shook under her gut-churning, ear-piercing shriek. It was the wind that could tear out a tree from the roots, that could hit the cliffs until they were bare stone, left empty under the sun. It was the wailing of the woods during a storm, the smell of ozone following a lightning strike. It was as ancient as the god's belly, digesting the centuries of sacrifices. It was, also, something completely young, like a demi-god born in the mountain, not long in this world. Left behind.

Her mother was always cagey over the identity of Bura's father. But when a small, young Bura heard once people gossiping that she was born of incest, she'd asked mother what the word meant.

"People think they are entitled to my secrets. But the only one that needs to know the truth is you," her mother had said to her that day, while the sun bathed them. She told her the story of how she was seduced by a wind, the same one that shaped the mountain they lived on. How it was a god so old no one

remembered it, not really a man, not a woman, but an unstoppable force. *"You are made of that power, never forget that,"* she said to Bura, while braiding her hair.

Years later, after her mother was long gone, she would learn how babies were made. And she would dismiss mother's magical tale of a wind coming down, lifting her up, up, over the cliffs and towards the skies, as a sort of a metaphor for sex.

But her blood remembered, and it soared free of any restraints, blowing at the polyps, crushing them under its blunt force. She couldn't see, but she felt the bursting, something warm and liquid—she hoped it was blood—spraying over her.

The loud thumps of something falling nearby joined the wailing of the wind and the grumbling of the earth.

"The cave's collapsing, we need to get away!" Dorja shouted in her ear. They were still completely blind, and the acidic smell was getting worse. The child was now between the two of them, unmoving, a heavy, limp weight in their arms. Without sight, she couldn't even start to guess the severity of its state. "I'll take the kid. You just go!"

Bura left the weight in the other woman's hands, unknowing if the child was alive or not. She turned in the opposite direction from the wall, trying to orient herself. Not with her eyes. But with her other sense, like Dorja had said. Towards the opening where the air slipped away, a beacon in the drowning darkness. Her wind rose at her back, giving a boost to her feet, making her almost fly amongst the shuddering ground collapsing in on itself. She didn't stop, didn't open her eyes, letting her body be taken, instead, by a current which was dragging her towards the surface. To the ghosts of the sacrificed, forever trapped.

Only there did she slow down, moving the pelt from her face to be able to look around. The dust of the debris was clouding the air, rocks falling down in chunks. Covering the empty skin shells, the clothes, bags, caps, armor; giving them a long-needed burial. Lost souls, only a thin mist hanging onto the wind, were getting extinguished one by one. Ivica's snowflake body was losing its form, the snow falling freely on the rocky ground, where it wouldn't have a chance to melt. She felt his smile and his whispered *thanks*, only as a vague memory of a time long gone. Dorja caught up to her; a bundle of a small, six or seven years old boy cradled at her chest, her face scrunched in question. Bura shook her head and followed her out of the cave.

They stood there, watching the collapsing cave in silent awe. The rocks burst from the ceiling, closing the opening one by one, raising the dust in a loud scream of an old thing dying.

And when the dust settled, it was as if the cave had never been there, its mouth sewn shut.

The child was alive. He was breathing, but his sickly pale skin was covered in sweat. Bura didn't recognize the boy, but she guessed, by his clothes, that he had to be native to one of the seven villages. She remembered the gathering in her own village before she'd run toward the woods, and wondered if it had anything to do with him.

"He needs care. We should bring him to your village as soon as we can," Dorja finally said. Her skin was now covered not only in crusted blood, but also in a thin coating of dust and smears so dark red they almost looked black. Bura looked the same, with tiny puncture wounds where the flailing polyp had caught her arm and bitten through her sweater and the coat.

She nodded, even though she wanted to say that they should bring him down the mountain, to a real doctor in town. That was the whole reason why she'd gone into the woods in the first place, which felt like ages ago. Without an automobile, it was still a difficult journey to take, especially with an injured child.

The woods lost their ethereal grandeur. They were just a collection of trees again, strong and tall, ordinary, that didn't throb with menace or hate. Just brown trunks growing towards the sky, their tops bowing under the steady coat of snow. Bura's heart was still beating hard, so she didn't even feel the cold of the snow making its fast descent.

Dorja took the lead, the child safe in her arms. Her naked body caught the snowflakes, her long black hair soon getting peppered with white. Bura trailed after her, feeling strangely calm. Her mind was devoid of feeling, like she was just on a stroll, drinking in the scenery. The whole time, though, she touched the small punctures on her arm, proof that whatever she'd just witnessed had truly happened.

And that, maybe, her mother hadn't lied.

That thought was the strangest of them all. It should mean something to her, to a child unwanted, unloved, but it didn't. She was a statue made of stone that fell from the cliff, smashing into a thousand pieces, unable to glue herself back together.

Time must've passed without her even noticing because, at some point, Dorja stopped, bringing her arm high in the air, her head inclined like she was listening to something Bura couldn't hear.

"The people are close," Dorja whispered, turning towards Bura. The child groaned in his sleep, his forehead wrinkled, but didn't move or open his eyes. Bura watched his form, so fragile and thin, clothes puckered with tiny holes, wondering if it was too late for him, if his organs are now just soup. How long did it take for a person to be eaten from the inside out?

"Did you hear what I said? There are people in these woods, looking for him, I reckon." Dorja put her arm on Bura's shoulder, nudging her.

"Yes. Sorry. Well, that's great. Isn't it?" Bura wasn't sure anymore, which way was the sky and which way was the ground. Wasn't certain if the numbness that had overtaken her limbs was a sign of tiredness, hurt, the cold or something else entirely.

Dorja's face was closed down, blank, her black hair now almost completely all white under the snow, but her eyes burned with the intensity of a thousand fireflies. "They can't find me with you. It would be hard to explain the naked woman in the forest. It will be hard enough to explain what's happened to the two of you, even without putting me in the mix." She squeezed Bura's shoulder, her mouth stretching in a lopsided, sad smile. "This is where we say goodbye."

Bura blinked, Dorja's words hitting her slowly, step by step, or a snowflake by snowflake which was catching onto her eyelashes. Her eyes watered up, and she had to swallow the disappointment, its taste like salt from unshed tears. "But, I don't..." *I don't even know what I'm supposed to do now after everything went wrong. I want to know who you are, learn more.*

She stood there, her mouth flapping open, too many words getting stuck in her throat, while Dorja simply pushed the child into her arms. Caught by surprise, Bura took him, this frail, light body, weighing almost nothing.

"You said you wanted nothing more than to show me the world," Bura said, "to explain to me what I want to know. What if I wanted to know more about you? Where you came from. What you like. What you actually do, and not just some vague stuff."

Dorja smiled sadly, wiping a snowflake off Bura's cheek, her palm so warm that Bura could get lost in her touch. "I'm sorry. But I can hear them getting closer, so I really need to go. But listen—follow this path, and you'll stumble upon your people." Dorja pointed with her arm at where she was supposed to go.

Bura struggled to untangle her thoughts, her emotions. Everything had gone wrong since she got into the forest, and it didn't stop. "But, will I see you again? Will you find where I live? Please, you can't just disappear." *As abruptly as you've shown up in the first place.* Saving Bura's life, helping her, guarding her. And now when they were close to Bura's home, Dorja was ready to go back to wherever she'd come from in the first place. Why did Bura expect anything different? Dorja had promised to get her out of the deathly trap but didn't show any inclination to become anything more than a short-lived ally.

Dorja worried at her bottom lip, her eyes clouded. "I did what I had to do. You're safe now," she said in the end, cementing Bura's fear. She had to blink away the tears, so she wouldn't show the hurt, even though she was sure her face was an open book. Hating herself for that, for showing she was pathetic enough to hope there could be someone in this world who wanted to be her friend. Granny was the only one who was truly there for her, and now she will maybe lose her too, through her own failures.

Turning away from Dorja, Bura abruptly went down the path the woman had shown her, not wanting to spend another minute on someone who didn't care about her, when the person who did was probably dying and needed her help.

She could feel a look burning through her skull when something fell on her face, almost obstructing her view. Something warm, leathery. Bura stopped at once, turning back towards Dorja, who was standing at the same spot where she'd left her. She moved away the pelt that managed to stay on her, somehow hooking at her chest, above the boy.

"Here," she called to Dorja. "This is yours."

Dorja blankly looked at her own wolf skin in Bura's outstretched hand. But she didn't move to take it back, frozen under the snow, almost looking like a sculpture made of ice. Bura frowned, stepping down on the frustration that was building up in her, a wind that shouldn't be let out. Seeing how the other woman wasn't moving, and with the child hanging in her arms in an uncomfortable position, Bura threw the pelt at Dorja. It awkwardly fell to the ground.

Dorja's eyes burrowed deep into Bura's mind. Like she didn't expect to get her skin back.

"Thank you," Dorja whispered, her voice a mix of regret and relief which Bura didn't have time to ponder over. She wanted to continue her dramatic walk, but there was one thing she still wanted to know.

"Would you at least tell me, before you go, what you meant by *doing what you had to do*?" She had her own suspicions, but wanted to hear it from the other woman.

Dorja turned her head towards the sky, snowflakes landing on her full lips and rosy cheeks.

"I'm a God's She-Wolf. I go where I'm sent." Her head swiveled down, her dark brown eyes so warm that Bura could almost imagine being near the flame of the hearth, even with the cold trying to invade every inch of her body. "You were in trouble, and a big one. Strayed onto a path you should've never found. My God... your other parent... tried to keep you away. When they failed, I was sent in to save you. They couldn't pass over, you see, because of the old agreement with the thing in the cave. But, in the end, you were able to save yourself. And even more than that. If they knew how strong you are... You managed to do something they couldn't have done. You destroyed that thing, freed the mountain."

Bura shouldn't have asked. The answer made her head hurt even more; some mysteries were better left undiscovered. She'd stumbled upon some ancient feeding site, in a story that wasn't even hers, but failed in what she'd set out to do. What did it matter if she killed one old god, leaving this mountain to the other, if she couldn't help her own grandmother? If, at the end of it all, she'd still be left completely alone?

It looked as if Dorja was waiting for Bura to say something else, but she stayed silent, her feelings too jumbled. After a few pointed moments passed, with the two of them just looking at each other and not moving in either way, Dorja took a deep breath and picked up the returned wolf skin, putting it back on with a bone-breaking sound that accompanied the process in reverse. Her human skin fell in strips from her crimson flesh, the guts hitting the snow with a hissing sound, the warmth of her insides turning into a white mist in the cold, snow-filled air. Her black hair disappeared under the black fur and her skull broke and rearranged until it had a muzzle again. Only her eyes stayed more or less the same.

The wolf stood over the steaming pile of her human blood and intestines, as big as a bear. And just like it had come, it went away, nodding its head goodbye before shifting its tail and running away. In the opposite direction from Bura, who stood there, half-buried under the snow, feeling nothing at all.

She stumbled upon her own villagers—a group of older and younger woodsmen alike, who cut down parts of the forest and sold it for warmth to the nearby towns. When they saw her—covered in tears, dust, blood, scrapes, bruises, and frost—holding an unconscious, bluish child in her embrace, their faces fell in shock and dread.

After that, everything was a whirlwind. They took the child from her arms, and a coat showed up on her shoulders, one of the men—old man Petar, a forty years old woodsman who sometimes worked with Granny—taking her under his arms, even though she didn't need to be helped. She didn't have it in her to object, either.

At some point, she told them how she went into the forest, how she got lost in the dark storm, how she found the kid in some sinkhole. She mumbled some nonsense about how she'd had to wrestle a wolf because, really, how else to explain so many dried, dark red spots covering her? Given how utterly trashed out she looked, it wasn't even that far-fetched. She burst into tears when the first houses of her village came into view.

Petar took her to her home, the others taking away the child somewhere else, a crowd grouping up in the center. One of the women had stayed with Granny, who was laying down on her cot, her eyes full of a watery fever. When she saw Bura, she reached out with her hand and Bura took it, kneeling down at her side. Granny shushed her and comforted her with warmed-up wraps on her chest and arms, smelling of strong alcohol—*rakija*—potatoes and vinegar.

Bura wept like that until someone helped her get out of her clothes and lean over the washbin, where she soon darkened the clear water, turning it black.

Someone called for the doctor for her Granny and the child Bura had found. He was from one of the other villages, lost the same day she'd gone into the forest. People were coming and going in their small home, helping out in a way they never did before. She saved a kid and suddenly, for a brief amount of time, at least, she wasn't a pariah anymore. Bura and Granny both knew this newfound status would not keep, but they enjoyed the perks while it did.

Bura wasn't certain she would be able to go through Granny's sickness on her own. The doctor came and went away—at the last moment, when the snow stopped falling, before all roads became impassable. He left some medication and harsh instructions but didn't look utterly convinced over

Granny's chances. He also examined Bura's wounds, but it only left him confused. He said she'd been lucky to stay alive, and that her skull must've been as hard as a rock. She hid her arm, knowing he would not be able to explain the indentations, and because she didn't want to be connected to the boy anymore than she already was. Knowing he must've had a quite interesting case with the kid.

The days came and went. Granny fought each of them to stay alive, while Bura helped her out. At night, she would sit at the hearth, a wolf figurine in her hands. One night, when Granny was better, Bura almost asked whether she knew who her father was. If she believed her mother's tale of a northern wind seducing her and leaving with a child. She kept it to herself in the end. Not wanting to hear what Granny had to say about any of it, especially now, when she knew the truth.

She burned the wooden wolf while Granny was sleeping, tears slowly trickling down her face. Dorja said it was a god that had sent her to guard Bura. But what good was to have a god for a father, when it didn't bring them food, water or shelter when he wasn't *there*?

Winter came into its full-blown strength. Snowstorms closed the school, the roads completely buried. People were hiding in the houses, burning through their wood piles. In the cellar, Bela was still giving milk; in the house, Granny was finally getting better. It was slowly getting back to normal in their home. Bura did most of the work but, from time to time, some woman from the village would come to check up on them.

Never Ika, though, and it was all for the better. Similarly, Bura wasn't sure what she would do to Nuncle when she saw him again, so she tried not to cross paths with him. There was one day, though, when the storm was so strong that the wind blew away the roof of his house.

So while it was not unusual to have an evening visitor, the person who knocked on their door one day shocked Bura, since she wasn't expecting to see her again, thinking their goodbye in the woods was the last time they'd speak and that it was where their story would end.

But there Dorja was, standing in the doorway with slight unease, looking awkward in human clothes. The object in her hands drew Bura's attention, and her eyes fell on it.

The red woolen hat, hand-knitted, lost that night in the woods.

"Can I come in?" Dorja asked, reaching out with the hat. Offering it back.

Bura blinked, believing that the she-wolf would disappear, that she wasn't actually there, but only a figment of her imagination. She hoped, of course, she did, unwilling to admit it, trying to avoid looking even more foolish than she was.

"Who's that at the door?" she heard Granny's voice at her back. Dorja cocked her head, her cheeks rosy, but her lips curved in her old, lopsided grin. There was something else in her eyes, a question, a worry. An uncertainty.

Bura swallowed through her joy.

"A friend," she called her answer, taking the hat back. Showing Dorja to come into the house. "I'm glad you managed to find my place."

"I'm glad, too," Dorja answered, even when they both knew it wasn't a problem for her.

Seasons changed, and with them, the weather. The old cow died in the spring, and then the grandmother followed her in the summer, her body getting buried behind her own house. Her granddaughter took out her stuff and didn't even try to sell the house. Together with the strange woman that had shown up the winter before, she ventured into the woods.

And never came back.

If the woodsmen believed they saw some strange cabin in the heart of the mountain, and a woman flying on the northern wind while a huge wolf howled below, those were only drunken tales. Nothing more.

AUTHOR'S NOTES

Thank you so much for reading this collection. Each of these five stories is dear to me and I'm glad I got to share them with you. (Also, I hope no one from the Istrakon convention organization will get mad at me—just like Jelena, I love Istrakon, which is the whole reason why I wrote a story featuring it. I'm pretty sure there are no ritual sacrifices going on in Istria, but you can never be 100% sure.)

Word of mouth goes a long way for small publishing. So, if you have the time, leave me a comment on Goodreads or social media—I would like to hear how you liked the book (or didn't), if there was something that spoke to you, which story you liked the most, would you rather get lost in the sea or in the woods... asking for a friend.

Big thanks to my editor and proofreader Vesna Kurilić. I couldn't have done this without her. And a very special thanks to Mojca Brenko-Puzak, who took an awesome photo for my cover. She was the one who got me interested in folk horror in the first place, and I hope that one day we'll get a chance to listen to her own folk horror lecture at a convention.

All of the locations mentioned here are real, except for the one in the story *The Rock at the Bottom*, which is loosely based on two Croatian islands—Korčula and Gubavac. I was inspired by a local story in one of the villages on Korčula, that people used to dump unwanted kittens on a small, barren island called Gubavac, close by.

On that note, the village Tzrni Dabar (Crni Dabar) and the other ones mentioned in the story *The Sound of Wind* truly did exist, but don't anymore. The conditions of life were too harsh, they were too remote and, with time, people slowly trickled out. The school in Ravni Dabar has nowadays been turned into a mountain hut, and I actually got an idea for the story when I visited there.

My father's family is from a region called Zagorje, hailing from a few of the villages near the town of Lepoglava. Jela's home, from the story *Mistress of Geese*, is based on my late grandparents' home. Also, I hate geese. They attacked me when I was a kid, and I've been afraid of them ever since. For me, the only good goose is the one on my plate.

I never specified where *The Lottery* takes place, but those who know something of Croatian geography could probably take a guess.

AUTHOR

Antonija is a Croatian writer, editor, cosplayer, and speculative fiction fan. Sometimes she reads, sometimes she writes, but mostly she procrastinates. Besides that, she loves to hold lectures and quizzes on various topics at conventions. She mostly writes folk horror and fantasy inspired by South Slavic folk tales, all of it queer. She's a co-editor at the online magazine for speculative fiction *Morina kutija* and a co-host of the Croatian podcast about writing and publishing, Mora FM.

You can follow her book ramblings at her haunted site, hauntednarratives.com, subscribe to her haunted newsletter, or check out her Twitter and Instagram @antonijamezni.

ALSO BY ANTONIJA

What Do Nightmares Dream of
a sapphic horror novella

It Eats Us From the Inside
queer aquatic horror novella

ABOUT SHTRIGA

Hidden Stories In Your Pocket.
Sci-fi, fantasy and horror on the go. Publishing your
daily dose of speculative fiction since 2020.

Visit
shtriga.com
for more information, or follow us
@shtrigabooks
on Twitter, Instagram and Facebook
for news, upcoming releases, giveaways and more

SHTRIGA